"But you'd always feel bad if you were the only survivor," Naomi offers. "Wouldn't you? Wouldn't you care about all the people who died, maybe even members of your own family?"

I'm not going to listen to this. I'm going to walk out of class right now and go home. I start to get to my feet, but Tasha and that stupid Sherman boy glance over at me, so I sit back down.

"Did you want to add something, Miss Deacon?" Mrs. Vargas asks.

Oh, I could add plenty! But I shake my head.

She goes on to someone else, but I'm too angry to pay attention. I want this class to be over, and I don't care if the building bursts into flame to end it. I don't care if the world flies apart! Then they'd find out what it's like to be left behind!

I can't get my breath . . .

★"Thesman handles the characters with sympathy and understanding. [Readers] will be carried through the book by the lure of their unresolved secrets. . . . This is a very fine book."
—*School Library Journal*, starred review

"Readers will be drawn into the complexity of Skylar's relationship with her sister and by the sensitive portrayal of a family struggling to cope in the face of a terrifying tragedy."
—*The Horn Book*

"This piercingly sad tale of a haunted family is assembled like a jigsaw puzzle, piece by piece. . . . One and a half hankies."
—*Kirkus Reviews*

OTHER PUFFIN BOOKS YOU MAY ENJOY

Calling the Swan

JEAN THESMAN

PUFFIN BOOKS

PUFFIN BOOKS

Published by the Penguin Group

Penguin Putnam Books for Young Readers,
345 Hudson Street, New York, New York 10014, U.S.A.
Penguin Books Ltd, 80 Strand, London WC2R ORL, England
Penguin Books Australia Ltd, Ringwood, Victoria, Australia
Penguin Books Canada Ltd, 10 Alcorn Avenue, Toronto, Ontario, Canada M4V 3B2
Penguin Books (N.Z.) Ltd, 182-190 Wairau Road, Auckland 10, New Zealand

Penguin Books Ltd, Registered Offices: Harmondsworth, Middlesex, England

First published in the United States of America by Viking,
a division of Penguin Putnam Books for Young Readers, 2000
Published by Puffin Books, a division of Penguin Putnam Books for Young Readers, 2002

3 5 7 9 10 8 6 4 2

THE LIBRARY OF CONGRESS HAS CATALOGED THE VIKING EDITION AS FOLLOWS:
Thesman, Jean.
Calling the swan / by Jean Thesman.
p. cm.
Summary: When Skylar goes to summer school and tentatively begins to
make some friends, she finally starts to get over the loss of her older
sister and its terrible effects on the whole family.
ISBN 0-670-88874-5 (hc)
[1. Loss (Psychology)—Fiction. 2. Grief—Fiction. 3. Sisters—Fiction.] I. Title.
PZ7.T3525 Cal 2000 [Fic]—dc21 99-053093

Puffin Books ISBN 0-14-230035-7

Printed in the United States of America

BOOKS BY JEAN THESMAN

Remembering Marianne

chapter
ONE

I don't want to start this day, but it began without my consent when the sun rose and I woke up. I wait, trying not to worry, until my alarm finally rings, and then I get up and dress. Morgan, our Siamese cat, watches in amusement when I fold my pajamas and put them on my closet shelf.

These days my bedroom is plain and bare, and I keep it carefully neat. Once it was quite different, colorful and cluttered, and Morgan could always find a nest for his nap on a pile of discarded clothes somewhere. But then, because I learned that I couldn't control my life, I controlled my room instead. First, I took down the poster Mom had made from her favorite snapshot of my sister and me when we were small, playing on the swings. Frozen forever, Alexandra soared higher, laughing, hair flying. I, the sedate one, swung close to the ground, afraid of falling.

Next I removed everything else from the walls and all the ornaments littering my dresser and desk. My bookcase contains nothing but books now. The TV and stereo are silent, unplugged. Everything is orderly. Quiet. Safe.

Today I leave here to start summer school.

At the other end of the hall in my sister's room, a stained glass sun-catcher dangles in the window and sheds a circle of bright color on the pale gray carpet. Inside the ornament's lead frame, a white swan floats on dark blue water where green branches trail narrow leaves. I close Alexandra's door behind me and step around the magical patch on the carpet.

"I don't think I can go," I tell her, struggling to talk in spite of the painful lump in my throat. "I can't do this."

She is curled up in the window seat with her long skirt tucked around her legs. "Nervous?" She closes her journal and puts down her fountain pen. "I thought you were feeling good about everything."

"I won't know anybody at summer school."

Alexandra looks out the window for a moment, and the sunlight illuminates her smooth skin, her long pale hair, and the thin fabric of her dress that is the color of the inside of a seashell. "You need new friends, Skylar," she says. When she looks back at me, she is smiling. "Come on. It'll be an adventure. And next fall you can take the design class you want so much, if you get English out of the way this summer."

"Maybe I won't like costume design," I argue. Whatever gave me the crazy idea that I would? I wonder as I fuss with my new shirt, tucking it in farther. The art teacher recommended me for the design class, but it conflicted with the rest of my schedule. I could sign up for it only if I cleared a space, and my advisor said English would be easy in summer school. I'd waited almost too long to make up my mind.

"And I hate this shirt," I say suddenly, irritably. "Look at it! Everybody will think it's ugly. And it scratches. I wish I hadn't bought it."

Alexandra laughs and shakes her head. Her clean straight hair ripples in the light like a pale liquid. "It's not a reason to stay home, if that's what you're after. Why don't you wear something of mine?"

"You know Mom would hate that," I say.

"Opa door BEN!" our little brother bellows, and he bangs on Alexandra's door with something hard.

"Ben, quit that!" I cry, and I pull the door open. "Did you hit the door with your dog? How did you get up the stairs?"

Our two-year-old brother holds a carved wooden dog in one hand. He scowls and marches in, followed by Morgan.

"Is everybody crabby this morning?" Alexandra asks.

Ben smiles angelically. "Ben wants up," he tells her, and he raises his chubby arms.

"You aren't supposed to sit on the window seats," I say, and I scoop him up.

"Ben DOWN!" he roars, and I put him back on the floor hastily.

"He's so hard to take care of," I complain. "I knew he'd be climbing over the stair gates before long. And he's always getting into things."

Ben, fair and blond like us, looks up and smiles at me. "Cookie?"

"No, breakfast," I say. "Let's go down and see what you did to the gates." I take him firmly by the hand and lead him out of Alexandra's room. The cat runs ahead of us, skittish, his tail stiff and bristly, prepared to do battle with imaginary baby dragons and make our way safe.

The gates at both the top and bottom of the steps are undamaged—and still closed. "Little beast," I mutter. Obviously Ben is better at climbing than I suspected. I find our mother in the kitchen and report the bad news.

"I didn't hear him!" she exclaims. She pushes back her untidy dark hair with its strange white streak. "What are we going to do with him?"

"Send him to Gran's until he's twenty-five," I say. Why had my parents decided to have another child when they were middle-aged?

"Skylar, sit down and eat," Mom says. "You've got plenty of time. Dad's left already, but I'll take you to school around nine-thirty."

I don't look at her, but instead sit down, taste my juice, and find it isn't as sour as it looks and smells. "I told you before that I'd take the bus," I say. I have to do this all by myself or it doesn't count. Gran and Alexandra understand this. Why doesn't Mom?

"It's two buses," Mom argues. "You'll have to transfer downtown, and I don't want you going alone. The school is in a bad part of town."

"Mother, I'm fifteen!" I say. "There's probably a bus stop across the street from the school. I'll be fine."

"No yelling," Ben says composedly as he helps himself to the cat's kibbles. I grab his hand and pry open his fingers.

Mom washes his hand and I eat quickly, hoping Ben will keep her busy long enough for me to escape from the house. But she is too smart for that.

"Ben and I will drive you to summer school just the way we drive you to high school. He'd be disappointed if you took the bus." She speaks in a firm voice to end the subject, the way mothers do.

"Ben doesn't care and I'm taking the bus," I say just as firmly, the way daughters do.

Gran comes in the back door then, with Ben's new curtains folded over one arm. "Who's going where?" she asks. Her white hair looks freshly cut and she is wearing it spiked again, something that always causes Dad to sigh. I suspect sometimes that he is uncomfortable with his tall, lanky mother and her imperative manners and uncommon opinions, but she suits the rest of us just fine.

Ben struggles to get away from Mom and runs straight to Gran. "Blankie?" he asks in his most beguiling voice. He recently pulled out all the stitches in his quilt. He already understands that Gran can fix almost anything.

"Nope," she tells him. "I told you I wouldn't fix it again. These are curtains for your room." She looks at me then. "Right. I remember. This is your first day at summer school. You'll have a great time and meet lots of new kids. If I'm not here when you get back, call me and let me know how it went."

She's provided me with a perfect exit. I bless her silently and hurry toward the front door. Mom calls me, but I rush out. I should have taken time to say good-bye, but I don't want to hear another version of the "you can't ride the bus" argument.

The blinds at the window of the house next door rise halfway when I reach the sidewalk. I know who is behind them but I won't look at the woman, the whisperer, the watcher. The lump is back in my throat. I run, in case Mom tries to follow me, and I don't slow down until I reach the end of the next block. There is no point in furnishing the neighbor with a scene.

The middle of June is often cloudy and cool in Seattle, but this morning the sun is out and the warm air smells of freshly cut grass and early roses. I don't see anyone I know, and I am grateful for that because I want this day to be as good as it can get. Of course, for that to happen I have to stop worrying about what the people at school might think of me, my hair, and my clothes.

Then there is the problem of not knowing where the classroom is. I can picture myself wandering around strange halls, like someone in a nightmare. I am doing this alone. Will everyone else there be with friends?

No, quit it, I tell myself. You're supposed to make yourself *stop* looking for trouble. You're supposed to say to yourself, "Why am I thinking about this *now?*" And if there isn't a good reason, you should move on to something else.

I wait at the bus stop with an old woman dressed in black and a boy about ten years old. Neither of them looks at me. Five crows sit in a big cherry tree in the yard across the street, and when I glance at them, they mutter among themselves. The boy folds his arms over his chest, as if he feels cold. Perhaps he is afraid the crows are discussing him instead of me.

When the bus comes, I let the others get on first, and I find an empty seat in the back. I've never been as adventurous as Alexandra. I've never wanted to charge out and take risks. But I can do this, I tell myself. I can go to summer school and meet new people, especially if Gran is on my side. I can stop waiting and hiding and wishing I were a child again.

I don't worry about anything—much—until I get downtown and have to transfer to the bus that will take me to Central High, a place I've never been, in a part of town I've only seen through car windows. The bus is coming and my hands start to shake. I wouldn't be this way if Mom hadn't been delivering me to school like a package for the last three years.

"Ask the driver where to get off," Gran told me once when I discussed this adventure with her, dreading it and wanting it, both at the same time.

I climb the steps and ask the scowling man behind the wheel, expecting him to shout or ignore me.

"Sit behind me and I'll tell you when to get off," he says. "But there's a dozen kids on the bus already. They'll be getting off at that stop. You can follow them."

I glance back once and see people my age talking to one another, even leaning across the aisle to make themselves heard. I sit behind the driver, hoping no one notices me.

My shirt is driving me crazy. Something—the label, maybe—is sticking into my back. The girls on the bus are wearing cotton T-shirts and shorts. What am I doing in a stiff shirt with a collar? I look ridiculous.

The bus labors uphill past restaurants, old apartment buildings, and shops selling things I can't imagine wanting, used furniture, window shades, and ugly sun-faded carpet. At each stop I think of getting off and finding my way home, maybe even calling and admitting that I can't do this. My stomach knots.

"Okay, get off here," the driver says.

I jump up, wanting to turn around and go home more than anything I've ever wanted.

Almost.

But I follow the other kids into the big gray stone building, past a husky security guard who smiles a fake smile at each of us while his small hard eyes examine us. I have my registration papers in my jeans pocket, with a small blue card that has my room number, 210, on it. If anyone wants me to prove who I am, I can do it.

Can't I? Can't I?

The main hall is gloomy, smells of disinfectant, and is lined with old brown metal lockers. I see offices behind dingy windows on either side of the broad staircase. The kids I followed scatter in all directions, as if they know where they are going. I am left standing before the stairs. I take out my blue card and my heart thuds. I can feel it all over my body.

I have plenty of time to find Room 210. Ten whole minutes. But I could turn around, go home, and admit my parents were right and Gran and I were wrong. Maybe Mom can arrange to move the school to our front yard. She probably wanted to do that anyway.

I climb the worn stairs, out of breath by the time I reach the landing because I am so scared. When I get to the top, I turn to the left and walk blindly down the hall. Finally I take control of myself and read the numbers on the doors. I am going in the wrong direction. Kids in the classrooms stare at me when I pass them for the second time.

Room 210 is halfway down the hall to the right. The door is open and I walk in, stiff and halting. The woman standing beside the desk says, "Good morning."

She can't be a teacher, I decide. The teachers I know wear jeans and sweatshirts. My regular school encourages everybody to dress casually, so that all of us, students, teachers, staff, and even the custodians, can be friends. Whoever thought that up has more trouble with reality than I do.

This woman standing by the desk wears a blue linen dress with a small white collar, and blue leather shoes. Her dark hair is short and neat. When she smiles, she has lines at the corners of her eyes.

"I'm Mrs. Vargas," she says. "Who are you?"

I consult my blue card, and the woman probably thinks I can't remember my name. Mrs. Vargas is the teacher, it says, so I must be in the right place. I clear my throat and say, "I'm Skylar Deacon."

She picks up a clipboard and reads something on it. "Interesting spelling of your name," she says.

"It's my mother's maiden name, but that's spelled S-c-h-u-y-l-e-r," I babble nervously.

"I like the new spelling," she says. "Put your registration papers in the box here and take any seat."

I fish the papers out of my pocket, drop them in the plastic box on her scratched wooden desk, and then look around the room for the first time. Half a dozen kids sit in back. Two boys look like athletes because their necks are thick and their shoulders are bulky. They glance indifferently at me and resume their whispered conversation. The two other boys sit many seats apart. One has long hair and the other has a tattoo on his neck. Ahead of them and sitting two seats apart, two girls look out the window at the twisted branches of old oak trees.

I start toward the row ahead of them, stumble over my feet, and bang against the corner of a desk so hard that I want to say "Ouch." I take the nearest seat before I do anything else stupid, and I think I hear one of the boys snicker.

I wish I were home, safe in my calm bedroom, with Morgan in my lap and a good book to read.

A dozen more kids come in and find seats. When the bell rings, Mrs. Vargas crosses to the door and closes it. The click is final. I am a captive.

"Okay, people," she says. "This is sophomore English, I'm Mrs. Vargas, and I'll call roll so we can all learn one another's names."

The two boys I'd thought were jocks keep whispering.

Mrs. Vargas picks up a book from her desk and drops it back on the bare wood.

"Let me set the scene for you," she says. She wears a small smile that reminds me of Gran's when she is annoyed. "In this class, *I* talk until I ask you to talk. If you talk when *I'm* talking, I'll ask you to leave and you won't get back in. Some of you need this credit, so think carefully before you strain my patience."

Everyone in the room is silent.

"Thank you," Mrs. Vargas says. "Now for roll call."

My ears are buzzing. I don't hear any of the names except my own. Miss Deacon, she calls me. Miss? I like that.

She picks up the book again. "Throughout the course, I'll read short stories and poems in class. Afterward, we'll discuss what you think the readings mean. That night you'll write approximately two hundred and fifty words expressing your thoughts on what you learned. Turn it in the next morning. You'll be graded on grammar, punctuation, and content. Neatness counts. Remember, I'm not looking for book reports or critiques on writing styles. I'm looking for ideas."

She has my attention. Will this be easier or harder than writing book reports?

"You won't be getting copies of the material I read," she goes on. "I want you to learn to listen, take notes, and then share your thoughts."

"Good," a boy says. "I don't want to read anyway."

Mrs. Vargas sighs. "Remember what I said about straining my patience. Interrupt me again at your peril."

"Sorry," the boy mutters.

She opens the book at a bookmark and says, "Many of you know Shirley Jackson's work because you've read 'The Lottery.' This is something different. It's called, 'The Very Strange House Next Door.'"

She moves behind her desk but she remains standing. I'm too nervous to hear the first few lines, but then I catch on. A woman in the story, who keeps explaining that she isn't a gossip, is gossiping about the new neighbors. She says terrible things about them, and before the story is done, she is responsible for them moving away.

The new neighbors are fairies. I add this to my notes and smile.

Mrs. Vargas is a wonderful reader. She is better than any actor on an audiobook. Sometimes what she reads is funny, and at first the class laughs only a little, as if they are afraid to make noise. But Mrs. Vargas's mouth twitches a bit, so I know she likes the laughter. After a while, the class laughs aloud.

When the story ends, Mrs. Vargas looks at her student list and says, "How about you, Miss DeAngelo? What did you think about this story?"

"Well," begins a small voice from the back.

"Please stand up so everyone can see you, Miss DeAngelo," Mrs. Vargas says kindly.

I turn with everyone else and look at one of the first girls I saw in the class. She is small and blond, and she looks like a member of the family described in the story, the one the horrible gossip called "foreigners."

She gets up awkwardly, blushes, and says, "I liked the part about the fairy kittens."

"What did you think about the family?" Mrs. Vargas asks.

"I wished they lived next door to me instead of the Newtons!" blurts the DeAngelo girl. "At least the fairies tried to help people."

Several people laugh.

"Mr. Clark?" Mrs. Vargas says.

I don't wanna hear about fairies," the brown-haired athlete says. He sprawls in his seat, grinning, challenging Mrs. Vargas.

"Please stand, Mr. Clark, so everyone can see you," Mrs. Vargas says.

The boy gets to his feet slowly, still grinning. "I said," he says in a raised voice, "that I don't wanna hear anything about queers." Now he is daring her.

I hear a couple of girls gasp. A tall, black girl murmurs, "Idiot." I turn to look at her and she meets my gaze. Her eyes are so dark they don't seem to have pupils. She nods briskly for emphasis, and I find myself nodding back.

Mrs. Vargas points a pencil toward the door. "You are excused, Mr. Clark," she says quietly with no expression in her voice. It is more unnerving than if she shouted.

"What do you mean?" he says. He is still grinning. The tall girl is right—he really is an idiot if he doesn't know he's in trouble.

"Leave the room," Mrs. Vargas says in that same deadly voice.

"I didn't talk when I wasn't supposed to!" he protests. His grin looks stiff now. "I got to have this class!"

"You may protest at the office," she says, and she looks at the student list again. He has been dismissed.

The entire class seems frozen, like people in a photograph. Then Mr. Clark begins a clumsy shuffle toward the door, muttering something I can't make out. I'm ready to feel sorry for him, but not quite, because I remember . . . other times.

Behind him, his friend says, "Well, hey. *Hey.*"

"Miss Deacon, what did you think?" Mrs. Vargas asks.

I feel as if I've received an electric shock. For a moment, I can't move. My heart is beating so hard that it moves my ugly blouse. My mouth is dry. Then I push myself to my feet and say, "I liked the family. They tried to help everyone. I don't know why that awful woman said those cruel things about them. It was a big loss when they left."

Mrs. Vargas smiles and I sit down, wishing I'd looked at my notes. I didn't make sense and now everyone is probably laughing at me.

"Does anyone know why the narrator said those terrible things about the strangers?" she asks.

Two hands go up. "Miss Johnson?"

Across the room, the black girl stands up. She is at least six feet tall and beautiful. "They were different, that's why," she says. "People never like strangers who are different."

Mrs. Vargas smiles again. "Do you agree with that, Miss Green?"

A girl as thin as I stands. Her brown hair curls around her face, and when she smiles, she has dimples. "I agree. People don't like others to be different, even if they aren't strangers. That's why we have race problems."

"Awww," complains a boy in the back. "Is this class gonna be one of those race things?"

"Please raise your hand after this if you want to speak," Mrs. Vargas tells him. "This class isn't about race. It's about communicating in the English language."

"I didn't mean to start anything," Miss Green says hastily and she sits down fast.

"Your comment was a good one," Mrs. Vargas says. "But what other things can cause people to resent their neighbors?"

She calls on a Japanese girl, who stands and says, "Religion."

Mrs. Vargas nods. "Mr. Parker?"

The boy with long hair gets to his feet. "Money." He sits down again, his face red.

Mrs. Vargas nods. "But what about the family in the story? Nothing was said about race or religion. Maybe they were more prosperous than their neighbors, but that didn't seem to be the main problem, did it? What do you think was the major issue?"

She calls on a plump girl with short red hair, who stands, checks her notes, and says, "They were mysterious. People don't like things they can't explain."

I grip my hands together in my lap and will my face to remain expressionless.

She is right. People hate what they can't explain. But something more was going on in the story. The strangers became victims—and eventually people hate the ones they've hurt, just to ease their own guilt. Gran told me that, and I try to remember it. I wish I truly understood it.

I desperately need to get out of the room, but there is no way I can leave without drawing attention to myself. This class is a mistake.

chapter

TWO

Mrs. Vargas moves about in front of the class as everyone talks. I see Gran's face in the small streaked window in the door and I stiffen resentfully. But at least it isn't Mom, watching me, worrying.

Gran disappears and now I can't concentrate. Why doesn't this class end? I look at my watch and at the clock on the wall, but they agree on the time.

Finally the bell rings, and Mrs. Vargas reminds us to turn in our papers the next day. "Remember, people," she says, "I don't want book reports and I don't want critiques. Write about what you think Jackson was really telling us. I want ideas and opinions."

Everyone else gets up, but I dawdle at my desk. I don't want the others seeing me collected like a crybaby kindergarten student by my grandmother.

Gran is nowhere in sight when I reach the hall, but I know she'll catch up with me before I make it to the sidewalk. I march down the stairs, keeping my eyes on my sneakers until I reach the first floor. There's Gran, talking to the security guard as if they've been friends forever. Her smile is confident and easy, his is tight and wary. I realize that he's hiding inside his uniform, hoping it gives him authority. Gran, like Mrs. Vargas, *is* authority and can afford to dispense genuine smiles freely. But still, I wish she hadn't come for me.

"At last!" Gran says, and she beckons. I join her reluctantly, looking around to see who is watching. No one.

On the way out, Gran starts explaining before I even ask a question. "It was either me or your mother," she says. "And I knew you'd rather I came. I convinced her that she was upsetting Ben with her pacing and worrying, and he'd yell his head off if she left him with me and came after you herself."

"I can take the bus home," I say miserably. "I'm not Ben's age."

"Of course you can take the bus," Gran says as she pads down the worn old stone steps next to me. "But you know how she can get. There's no reasoning with her. Just don't start in when you get home and chances are she'll get used to the idea a lot sooner."

"It's been years!" I say. "She's been doing this for almost *three years*."

Gran's car is parked a block north, she says, and I walk the rest of the way in silence. But Gran, being Gran, chatters on and on. "Look at this tearoom, Skylar. I've been here twice. It's the loveliest place, with gorgeous wood paneling and thick carpets. You and I'll have lunch here one of these days."

I consider a whole summer of being fetched and carried by the adults in my family, and I want to scream.

"Okay, Gran," I say, worn out with the hopelessness of the whole thing.

On the way home, we stop at the intersection by a small, peaceful park, and I see Alexandra moving behind the trees. But no, it's not her. It's another girl in a long, pale pink dress that shimmers and flutters among the drooping green branches.

I almost remember something, but then I forget again.

We hear Ben yelling when we get out of the car at home. He's with Mom in the backyard, hanging on to the garden hose with both hands. He's completely soaked.

"I don't know how he learned to turn it on," Mom says when she sees us coming through the side gate.

"He's smarter than he lets you know," Gran says. "Maybe he doesn't talk much in sentences the way the others did, but don't forget what happened to the old clock when he got hold of it."

"Gran, taking a clock apart doesn't mean he's smart," I say. "It just means he's busy."

Morgan, the cat, is wet, too, and he looks disgusted. I carry him into the house, leaving Gran to deal with Mom and Ben and the latest mess. "I think you can get locks for outdoor faucets," Gran is telling Mom as I let the screen door bang behind me.

I dry the cat with one of the new towels I take from the downstairs bathroom and then run upstairs to tell Alexandra about summer school.

For a moment I think she is reading in the window seat, but she is writing again. She looks as tired as I feel, but she smiles when she sees me. "How did it go?" she asks.

I sit on her soft pink bedspread. The room smells faintly of her vanilla and strawberry cologne. She hung her copy of the poster over her bed, and my breath catches in my throat when I see her on the swing, flying, long hair spread like wings. "I like the teacher," I say. "She already threw one boy out."

Alexandra laughs. "Is that a reason to like her? She sounds mean."

I tell her everything, and by the time I'm done, Alexandra wants to read "The Very Strange House Next Door."

"I have to write a paper about it," I say. "Or rather, what I think about being around strange people. Mrs. Vargas wants ideas from us."

"That's a switch from book reports," she says. "Well, you're good at that kind of thing."

"I don't think so," I say slowly. Hasn't she noticed? I'm not good at anything anymore.

"Did you like the kids?" she asks.

"They seem okay," I say. "Mrs. Vargas calls us 'Miss' and 'Mister.'"

Alexandra nods approvingly. "So everybody's all grown up. The class sounds as if it's in an old-fashioned private school somewhere."

She's right. I hadn't thought of it that way before. "The class is quiet," I say, and that seems even more remarkable to me now. "People stand up when they're called on, they don't just yell things from their seats. Well, they don't do it more than once."

"See if you can go to that school all year long," Alexandra says, grinning.

Ben is upstairs in his bedroom now, banging rhythmically on his xylophone, singing, "Bye-bye Gran, bye-bye Gran." Obviously Gran's left for home.

"Mom says she's going to start Ben on piano lessons when he's three, like she did us," I say wryly.

Alexandra shakes her head as Ben, down the hall, switches to pounding on something else and yelling unintelligibly. "Maybe she can enroll him in something a little more physical. How about Hockey for Tots?" Alexandra's boyfriend plays hockey. She actually likes watching. I think it's too violent.

"I'd better go," I say, and I slip out the door and go to my own room. The cat has curled up on my bed and is licking a paw fastidiously.

"Don't blame me," I say as he fixes his crazy cross-eyed gaze on me.

Mom stops in my open doorway, holding clean clothes for Ben. "He goes through things faster than I can run the washer and dryer. Gran says you had a good time in class. I hope you understand about her picking you up. The bus—"

"Was just fine," I finish as I begin unbuttoning the shirt I've come to hate. "The second bus was full of kids going to the school. I'm perfectly safe, and now I know my way around so I won't get lost." I look sharply at her. "I was embarrassed, seeing Gran waiting for me. Nobody else had to be picked up by a grown-up. You're not supposed to be doing these things—keeping after me like this. You're not!"

Mom studies my bare wood floor as if she hasn't seen it before. "We have to use common sense," she says.

"That's what I'm trying to do," I say as I yank off the shirt. "I hate this thing. I should have listened to you when you said the cloth was too heavy."

Mom reaches for it, distracted. "Let me run it through the wash a couple of times and see if that softens it. But if you hate it, you don't have to wear it."

I pull on a T-shirt and sit at my desk. "I've got homework so I should get started," I say, wanting to put an end to the conversation.

"Already?" she asks. "Okay, I'll let you get to it."

I sit at my desk, turning pages in my notebook until she dresses Ben in dry clothes and takes him downstairs again.

What am I going to write? How would I feel about strange people living next door?

Suddenly I laugh angrily. Maybe I should go next door and ask those people how they feel about living across the fence from *us*. Except they made sure we already know.

What did the people in class talk about this morning? It is hard to concentrate. My mind skips around, remembering only bits and pieces of the conversations. Money. Race. Religion. Those things can cause problems with neighbors.

Mysterious people can be problems, too, one girl said.

I grip a pencil hard and shake my head. No. I won't write about that.

I'll write about how people discriminate against one another because of religion. That will be safe enough.

I still can't think of anything to put down on the blank paper, so I go back to Alexandra for help, and she, as usual, comes up with the perfect idea.

"Remember when we lived in Portland, and there was that old woman down the street who we thought was a witch?" she asks. "Or at least we used to talk about her as if she were."

"I remember that," I say. "You never told anyone what we made up about her, but I told my friends and you got upset with me. You said if you talk about things with people outside the family, they can come true. You used to be so superstitious." Now it seems strange to me that she would be the superstitious one when she was also the brave one.

21

"We were mean kids sometimes."

"You mean *I* was a mean kid," I say. "At least that time. My friends and I yelled things at her when we passed her house. She got so mad at us."

The woman was more than angry. I remember it all now. Sometimes she looked at us as if she was afraid of what we might do to her. We wouldn't have hurt her! We were just . . . we were hating our victim. Hating her was easier than feeling guilty.

I shake my head to clear it of poison. "People act on what you tell them, just the way it happened in the story. I can write about how people don't always think for themselves. The other girls and I kept making up bigger and bigger stories about the woman."

"Be sure to say that you and your friends were only little kids then," Alexandra says. "You want to make a point of that."

I return to my room, satisfied until I recall that I was upset in class because I remembered the people who hurt *me*—because they were so willing to be cruel.

No! I won't think about them now, I tell myself. This is not the right time. I get to choose the times I think about people like that, and this is not the right time.

I bend over my desk and begin writing. Later, before dinner, I'll use the computer in the den and type a final copy. Maybe I'll get a good grade, especially since neatness will count.

I like Mrs. Vargas.

Dad comes home from his office early and corners me in the den, just as I'm finishing.

"How was summer school?" he asks as he settles himself in the armchair by the window. He looks so old now, so tired all the time. His thick brown hair has turned thin and gray, and there are heavy lines on his face.

"Summer school was fine," I say. "I like the teacher and the kids seem okay." I tell him about the story.

He smiles, but when I finish, he says, "You shouldn't have taken the bus to school. You frightened your mother."

"I *should* have taken the bus," I argue. "I'm ready for that and everything went just fine. The bus stops across the street from the school, and there were a lot of kids on it. The bus going in the other direction stops in the next block. I saw the place when I got there this morning. It's in front of a grocery store with all sorts of people going in and out, Dad!"

He shifts uncomfortably in his soft chair. "Skylar . . ." he begins.

"Let me grow up," I say firmly, quietly, even though I'm not sure I mean it. It just seems to be the right thing to say now. I know I can't back down on anything, not even a little bit, or I'll find it too easy to give up. I don't look at him again but return to work. He gets up stiffly, as if he aches all over, and he leaves.

After dinner, Mom and Dad tell me they have decided to let me take the bus. Mom is pale, and the circles under her eyes are worse than ever.

"I'll be fine," I say. "Thanks." But their worry follows me upstairs, through the two gates and into my room. I can almost see it hanging in the air like a damp mist that makes it hard to breathe.

I go to bed early, after I put out a T-shirt and jeans for the next day and tuck my assignment in a new folder. Sometime during the night

CALLING THE SWAN

I dream of a swan swimming away from me across a lake that looks like a black mirror. I call to it—it has a name I can't remember the moment after I say it—but the swan rises suddenly, scattering silver drops that fall on the dark water, leaving round marks like polished coins. I lie awake until dawn.

I ride downtown again, and I bring a book to read this time. While I wait for the transfer bus, I smile at a girl I saw yesterday, but she doesn't smile back. Perhaps I wouldn't smile at someone waiting here either, I tell myself. It doesn't matter. When the bus comes, I get on, choose a seat, and open my book, although I can't concentrate well enough to read.

In class, I see four new students. But three of the people who were here yesterday are missing, among them the friend of the boy who was asked to leave.

I sit at the same desk. Mrs. Vargas collects our papers, then writes the word *verb* on the board. Someone in the back of the room groans. We're going to have a grammar lesson.

But Mrs. Vargas has a surprise for us. Halfway through the class, she picks up the stack of papers we left on the corner of her desk. "Let's hear what some of you had to say about our discussion yesterday," she says. "I won't read your names, just the papers."

I cross my fingers until I learn that the first paper isn't mine. It isn't very good, but the student makes a point at the end about the stupidity of hating people because they have more—or less—money than we do. "What if there were a flood and everybody lost everything?" Mrs. Vargas reads. "Is that what it would take to make everybody equal?"

She puts down the paper and looks around. "Comments, class? Is that what it would take?"

The tall black girl raises her hand confidently.

"Miss Johnson, what do you think?" Mrs. Vargas asks.

"Even if everybody lost everything, some people would still pick on other people," the girl says. "I don't think the problem would go away, just because everybody became poor all of a sudden. There are still all those other problems."

Mrs. Vargas calls on Mr. Parker, the boy with long hair. He stands and says, "Some people are just rotten. The woman in the story, the one who said she wasn't a gossip but she was, she's just rotten. She liked what she was doing."

He'll think *I'm* rotten, if Mrs. Vargas reads my story. But I was just a kid then! Why did I write about the old woman? Why did Alexandra suggest it to me?

The boy sits down, folding his legs in a way that reminds me of a grasshopper. He glances at me as if he hears my thoughts. I look away guiltily.

Miss Green, who has dimples, offers the opinion that people wouldn't be that way if someone loved them. Miss Johnson, resting her weight on one narrow hip, contradicts her, saying that some people are born mean and never change.

Mrs. Vargas knows how to turn things around and avoid an argument. She calls on people who've been sitting there in silence, probably doing the same thing I've been doing—praying that she won't notice us.

"Mr. Sherman, what do you think about the idea that some people are born mean?" she asks the boy with the tattoo on his neck.

Wasn't it a snake tattoo yesterday? I can't remember. Now it seems to be an elaborate and colorful design, almost a scrap of an embroidered ribbon. I don't hear what he says because I'm staring at his neck and wishing I sat behind him so I could study it.

The last paper Mrs. Vargas has time to read is mine. I sit, miserable, while she goes through it. Can't I write any better than that?

"What do you think, class?" Mrs. Vargas asks at the end.

Miss DeAngelo offers the news that she did something that bad when she was seven years old. "But it's not the same thing as the woman in Shirley Jackson's story," she says. "Kids do stuff they shouldn't, but it's not like being an adult and knowing better."

Does anyone suspect that I wrote the paper? I'm afraid to look around. My face is on fire and my hands shake a little, so I press them together. When the bell rings, I shoot out of my seat.

I'm halfway down the hall when Miss Johnson catches up with me. "Slow down!" she says, laughing.

I look up at her because she's so tall. What does she want?

"You wrote the last paper, didn't you?" she asks, getting right down to business in a way that Gran would certainly like.

I hurry down the stairs, not wanting to be rude but not wanting the conversation, either. "How did you know?" I ask after I realize that I can't lose her.

"You blushed a lot," she says. "Don't feel bad because you told your friends that the old woman was a witch. I probably would have done the same thing. But I've got a sister, and she's like yours—what's her name? Oh, yes, Alexandra. My sister is practically perfect, too. Doesn't it make you mad?"

Alexandra never makes me mad, but this isn't the time to argue with a stranger. "Sometimes," I say.

"Are you taking the bus downtown?" she asks.

We're in the main hall now, approaching the security guard, who is deep in serious conversation with two boys who can't be old enough for classes here.

"Yes, are you?" I ask.

"No, I walk home," she says. "What's your first name?"

"Skylar," I say. It's only polite to ask hers, too.

"Tasha," she says. "My sister's name is Olivia. Old Miss Perfect."

We stand outside the building, awkward and strange, yet smiling at each other. "I'm crossing the street here," she says. "See you tomorrow."

"See you," I say, and I hurry past the front of the old building, cross to the bus stop in front of the grocery store, and stand at the edge of the group of waiting people.

"Hi," a girl says behind me. I turn, wondering if she's talking to me.

Miss DeAngelo smiles at me. "I guess we take the same bus," she says. "Do you transfer downtown?"

I nod. "I go north," I say.

She shrugs. "I go south. My name's Naomi. I can't get used to being called Miss DeAngelo. That makes me sound like my old aunt."

"I'm Skylar," I say.

"I know," she says. "I heard you tell the other girl. She's sure tall."

"I wish I were," I say.

After that we ride for ten minutes making small talk, and then we separate to catch other buses and go home. I hug myself while I wait. I made two friends.

Well, almost. But even that counts for something. I can't wait to tell my sister.

chapter
THREE

Mom is resting on the lawn swing in back when I get home. She's been reading, or trying to. There's an open book lying facedown on the table next to an empty juice glass. When she sees me, she sits up.

"Are you all right?" she asks a little too loudly. Her worry shows in her face and her hunched shoulders. She looks as if she is awaiting a blow. *Oh, Mom.*

I sit in one of the prim little iron chairs at the table. "I'm *fine*," I say. "I still like the class and I'm even making friends." Well, that's an exaggeration, but who cares?

She nods and picks up her glass, then looks surprised because it's empty.

I jump up from my chair. "I'll get you something. Do you want water? That awful health drink you like?"

Mom smiles a little, and for a moment she looks younger. "You could try that drink yourself," she says. "It's full of good things."

"Like celery juice and ground-up brussels sprouts," I say.

She raises a thin hand in protest. "Oh, it doesn't have brussels sprouts in it. But yes, I would like some, with ice, please."

I take her glass into the house. Ben trots into the kitchen in his underwear, dragging his green blanket behind him. "No nap for Ben!" he yells on his way to the back door. "No, no, no."

I hear Mom say, "Not already!" She lets him take naps on the couch in the family room sometimes. Obviously he isn't going to cooperate today.

I fill her glass with the yellowish green juice and dump four ice cubes in it. By the time I get back outside, Ben has climbed up in the swing with Mom and is arranging the grubby blanket over them both.

"Crabby take a nap," he tells her seriously.

Mom bursts out laughing. "He said a whole sentence."

"And what a sentence," I say as I put the glass down on the table near her. "Wouldn't you just know it would be something like that?"

I leave them there and go up to Alexandra's room. As I enter, I catch the sweet scent of her cologne. "Mm, nice," I say. "Guess what? Ben just said a whole sentence. He brought his blanket to Mom and said, 'Crabby take a nap.'"

"He's been putting strings of words together for a couple of weeks," she says. "He even told Morgan he was a jerk."

I laugh. "He listens to Dad grouching at the TV. We're lucky that 'jerk' is the worst thing he says."

"How was school today?"

"Good," I say. "Two girls talked to me for a little while."

Alexandra nods. "But don't get too hopeful right away, though. You know how things can turn out. Sometimes everything seems great, but then the person turns out to be . . ." She hesitates and then smiles. "A jerk."

I don't return the smile. "I thought you said I needed new friends."

"You do. Just don't get carried away. Be careful."

I don't want to dig into that too much. "Mrs. Vargas is nice," I say. "This is the first time I ever really liked an English teacher. She even makes grammar painless. Well, sort of painless."

On my way out of her room, I can hear Mom and Ben downstairs in the kitchen. Apparently the nap idea didn't work out. Ben is yelling, "Gimme gimme!" and Mom is saying, "Now you just *wait*."

Gran wanted me to call her, so I use the hall phone. "I had a pretty good time today," I tell her.

"How was your mother when you got home?"

I hesitate. "Not happy about it."

Gran hesitates a moment, too, then says, "I'll come over and give this my official seal of approval. Let's keep everything upbeat."

When I run back down to the kitchen, I find Mom and Ben sharing a peanut butter sandwich. "Do you want one, Skylar?" Mom asks.

"I'll fix it," I say. She's put the bread in the refrigerator and the peanut butter in the bread drawer. Oh well. It could be worse. It's *been* worse.

"I'm sorry you're still worrying about me," I say a little louder than I need to. "But I managed everything just fine today. Just like everybody else."

Mom's eyes fill with tears and she brushes them away on the back of one hand. "I can't help worrying."

Okay, what am I supposed to do? Ask her to drive me back and forth to school so she won't worry and make herself sick over it? It isn't a trap she's set for me. She isn't like that. But somebody has to do something. Has Mom forgotten that I'm not like Alexandra? I don't fly on swings, I barely skim the ground.

"I'm only gone for the morning," I say, even though I've begun losing my courage again because she can't find hers.

Ben, finished with his sandwich, carries his plate to the sink and casually tosses it in. It's plastic, so it bounces.

"Good boy Ben," he announces cheerily. He has peanut butter around his mouth.

I mop him off with a damp paper towel and kiss his face soundly. "I love you, Ben," I say, suddenly desperate and scared. "You really are a good boy."

"My pants are wet," he says conversationally, and he takes my hand, intending to lead me to the hall door.

"Oh, wonderful," I say. "Another sentence, and it's just the sort of thing we want to hear when we're all at the store."

Mom, done crying now, says, "That's better than what you said in the drugstore after you learned to sound out words. I knew I shouldn't have taken you down the aisle where the condoms were."

She leads Ben down the hall to the bathroom. The phone rings then, and I pick up the kitchen extension.

"I'm in my car, right around the corner," Gran says. "Everything okay?"

"Not too bad," I say, hating myself for needing her.

There's a moment of silence, and then she says, "Don't feel pressured."

I hang up after she does. Morgan strolls to the door, cries hoarsely once and sits down. I let him out and watch him find a sunny place to curl up for his nap. If only Ben took care of himself as well as the cat.

Okay, I'll forget the bus and let Mom or Gran take me back and forth to school. That little bit of independence isn't worth the price.

Gran comes in then. She hugs me hard and must read my expression, because she says, "Don't even think about giving up. Don't change anything. You need a little freedom, but your mother needs something else. I'll take care of it. Don't you have something to do in your room?"

"I thought I'd read outside," I say.

"Good idea. Now where are they?"

I tilt my head toward the hall door. "In the bathroom."

Gran nods and then says loudly, "Hey, people, is anybody in the mood for ice cream at that outdoor place next to the mall?"

Ben, roaring, "Gran, Gran," rushes into the kitchen. Mom follows, holding Ben's shoes and socks.

"That sounds like a wonderful idea," she says, but she doesn't look as if she means it.

"I've got a lot of reading to do," I say. "See you later, Gran." I dart outside before Mom can protest. I'm not carrying a book, but no one seems to notice.

What will Gran say to her? Oh, don't hurt her feelings. Don't nag her. She's really trying as hard as she can.

They leave, and I sit on the stiff little chair, watching crows in the maple tree. Are these the same ones I saw at the bus stop? There are only four this time, and they sit quietly, studying me. Then one drops down to a lower branch and caws. The other three immediately raise a racket that must be heard all over the neighborhood. Where is the fifth one? I look behind me and all around, then realize how silly I'm being.

But they make me nervous. I remember Dad telling me once about a crow that attacked him when he was mowing the lawn. I go back to the kitchen and fix another sandwich, then read the entertainment section of the morning paper Mom left on the counter.

It would be fun to go to a movie with friends. Maybe Tasha and Naomi would like to do that someday. We could have lunch and then go to an afternoon show downtown.

Stop it, I tell myself. Don't count on anything. Remember what Alexandra says.

Mom doesn't mention my taking the bus and worrying her. Whatever Gran told her has worked. At least for a while. Nearly everything works for a while.

The next day in class, Mrs. Vargas gives us another grammar lesson, this time based on the most common mistakes we made on our papers. She's animated and funny when she writes out examples on the board. Most of the people pay attention, but Mr. Fisher, a boy wearing a denim jacket and a watch cap pulled down to cover his ears, openly sleeps through most of the period. She leaves him alone until after the bell rings, and then she bends over him and says something so softly that I can't hear. She doesn't look angry.

Tasha and Naomi walk out of the building with me. "When is she going to read another story?" Tasha asks. "I wish she'd do it every day."

"This isn't story time in grade school," Naomi says. "But wouldn't that be fun? I'd rather listen to her than talk about stuff afterward. Listening is easier than thinking."

Tasha shouts out laughter and other people turn to stare at us. They laugh, too, without knowing what's funny.

Four girls have made themselves comfortable under one of the ancient trees on the school's front lawn. They're passing around a bag of doughnuts, and my mouth waters, watching them.

"Oh, my favorite food!" Naomi says when she sees them. "Where do you suppose they got the doughnuts?"

"From the grocery store across the street," Tasha says. "They have a great bakery."

"We should do that sometime," Naomi says.

"I've got a piano lesson at one," Tasha says. "But I'd like to do it some other day."

Naomi looks at me hopefully. "How about you, Skylar?"

"I can't today, either," I say. "I have a dentist appointment."

That's a lie, but I hope that she can't tell. I don't want to hurt her, and I want to be asked again, because maybe I'll have enough courage next time. Maybe Mom will have enough courage.

"We'll definitely do it sometime soon," Tasha says.

Naomi looks relieved. Is she afraid that she's been too friendly all of a sudden?

Maybe she has been.

I smile at her and tell her that her idea is a good one. I don't want anyone else worrying about the stupid things that worry me.

Gran takes me to the rectory across town, as usual. Every Wednesday I have an appointment with Father Carrington, the priest at the Episcopal church where we started going before Ben was born. He waits for me as he always does, inside the door of the old brick building that has ivy climbing lovingly to the roof. We walk back to his office together, not speaking. I like the silence in this building. I'm sorry we have to disrupt it with talking.

Outside his window, a willow tree bends low over a bed of blooming scarlet rhododendrons. I've watched the tree and the shrubs here through all the seasons, and I know them better than I know the things growing in my own yard.

I take my usual seat opposite his desk and turn in it so that I face the window. "The flowers look great," I say politely.

"Those are the last of the late rhododendrons," Father Carrington says as he sits down behind his desk. "But the roses are coming along."

His hair had been red, he told me once, but it faded to gray. His beard is still red, though. He wears a white T-shirt tucked into baggy tan pants. I always feel better when he wears a black suit and white clerical collar, but I don't tell him that. He probably thinks I feel more comfortable if he looks casual. I don't. How can I rely on someone who doesn't look any different from anybody else? How can I tell people apart unless they dress to fit their roles? But even then, how can I tell good people from bad? Light from dark? Flying from falling?

Father Carrington has a small list on his desk, carefully centered on an untidy stack of papers. We're going to do the "What are your goals?" thing again. Inwardly, I sigh.

"I made a list of the ideas we shared last week," he says. "I didn't want to forget any of them."

He means that he doesn't want me to pretend that *I* forgot. I managed to conveniently forget a lot of things in these last long years. I suspended everything I could and now I do my best to ignore everything else. I want to sleep on the swing—and not know when I fall.

"The most important idea was taking the bus to summer school," he says. "How has that worked out?"

"I do it, every day." I speak to the tree. Father Carrington is used to being left out.

"Are you comfortable going alone?"

I nod. "It works out just fine."

"How about your mother? How does she feel about it now?"

A muscle at the side of my mouth twitches. I wonder if he sees it. "She doesn't like it, but she's letting me do it." I swallow hard and go on. "When I got home today, she fussed about it a little."

Both of us wait a while before I can finish. "Gran came over and took Mom and Ben out for ice cream. I don't know what she said to Mom, but things were better afterward."

"Your grandmother's strong, like you," he says. "Strong and responsible."

"My mother is responsible, too!" I say sharply.

"Yes," he says calmly. I hear the whisper of moving paper. "Then you said you might get out your sketch pad and do some drawing this summer."

"I will," I tell the tree. "But I've been busy. I've had homework already."

"How did it go?"

The tree waits. "I made an idiot out of myself," I say. "Mrs. Vargas read my paper to the class. She didn't give my name, but one of the girls knew it was mine."

"Oh?" he asks. "How did that happen?"

"She said I blushed. That gave me away."

He says, "You have fair skin. It's nothing to worry about. What did you write that made you uncomfortable?"

I tell him about Alexandra and me and the old woman. Now the story sounds even worse. "I'm sorry I did it," I say sincerely. "It was mean."

A breeze agitates the willow branches.

"You were only a little girl at the time. I don't think it's the end of the world. However, the woman was probably relieved when you moved away." He rattles the list and says, "You also were considering taking piano lessons again this summer."

"One of the girls in my class had a piano lesson today," I say.

The tree seems interested in that and lowers a branch toward me, encouraging me to go on.

"You wish you'd gone with her to meet her teacher?" he asks.

"Maybe. I don't really know," I say slowly. I liked practicing. I *loved* it. And I was good, almost as good as Alexandra, who is three years older than I. Is this a good thing to tell the priest, who is also my counselor? No, it sounds too much like bragging.

"But you haven't said anything to your parents yet," he prompts me.

"Not yet. There was the problem about my taking the bus. I didn't want to start any other complicated conversations with them."

"You think there would be a problem if you asked for piano lessons again?"

The tree leans in a bit, waiting for my answer.

I can't speak. My tongue sticks to the roof of my mouth. Alexandra and I always went to the piano teacher's studio together, and she waited while I had my lesson. Then I waited for her. That's how it was, after we moved to Seattle when I was eight. When we lived in Portland, our teacher had come to the house.

The tree straightens, not satisfied with what I'm thinking.

I sit a little straighter, too.

"I'm already pretty busy," I say. "There's only so much I can do over the summer."

"You don't feel as if you have time for piano lessons right now?"

I know what he's trying to do. He wants to keep me out of Alexandra's room. He tries it every once in a while. There's no point in arguing with him about it, but I wish I'd never told him in the first place that I rely on her for advice.

"I don't have time for piano lessons this month," I say. "Maybe I'll do it in July."

The tree nods, pleased.

"How is Ben?" Father Carrington asks. "I like looking out on Sunday mornings and seeing him."

"Mom should put him in the nursery with the other little kids," I say. "He makes so much noise, and he bothers people."

"Your mother isn't ready for that yet."

I turn to look at him and catch him rubbing his temples gingerly.

"But Ben is ready," I say stubbornly. "He'd love being with the other kids and he wouldn't be pestering the grown-ups."

"I think Sunday services can withstand the onslaught of Benjamin Matthew Deacon," Father Carrington says, sounding amused.

I remember suddenly the afternoon Ben was baptized. My family and my uncle and aunt from Portland, who were Ben's godparents, were the only ones in the big, echoing church. Father Carrington had decided that this would be better for Mom.

Oh, she's so fragile! She gets thinner every week. She never wears makeup, she never gets new clothes, and she cuts her own hair without caring, as if it irritates her and the only thing that matters is getting it away from her face. She's waiting. We're all waiting, and it's been nearly three years!

"Yes," says Father Carrington.

Have I spoken aloud? I shut my eyes and bend my head. How awful. I can't tell the difference anymore between thinking and talking. No wonder I have to see him every week.

"You're a good daughter," he says. "I see more of your grandmother in you all the time—that ability to solve problems, the strength and humor, the bright intelligence."

I want to tell him he's wrong. He's talking about Alexandra, not me.

A small bird flutters among the willow leaves. If I had wings, I could join him and look in the window and wonder about the people trapped inside.

"I'm doing the best I can," I say.

"And your sister?" Father Carrington asks slyly.

The muscle beside my mouth twitches again. Why is he doing this to me?

"Leave Alexandra out of it," I say. "She has nothing to do with *anything*."

"Perhaps we'll explore that, when you're not hanging about in her room so much," he says.

I glance at him, startled, and see that he's put the list away. He raises his eyebrows innocently.

We spend the rest of my appointment talking about my diet. Father Carrington is big on eating healthful foods. He even approves of Mom's favorite drink.

He walks me to the door when we're finished, and Gran is waiting in her car in the parking lot. He strolls over to the driver's side and asks her something about the Altar Guild. I climb into the passenger seat, not really listening, my cheeks still stinging over what he said about hanging about in Alexandra's room. I'm always welcome there! I'm not pestering her!

"So how did it go?" Gran asks as she drives me home.

"The same way it always does," I say, and then I add angrily, "he should prune his willow tree. It's hanging down on the rhododendrons. It looks awful."

Gran doesn't respond. I stare ahead, my fists clenched in my lap.

chapter
FOUR

At home, Mom is slicing tomatoes in the kitchen and Ben is coloring around the edges of his paper, leaving red wax lines on his highchair tray. He's frowning and the tip of his tongue is sticking out of one corner of his mouth.

"Why don't you color *on* the paper?" I ask him.

"Nope," he says without looking up.

"Never disturb an artist at work," Gran says as she pulls a chair away from the table and sits down. "Nora, do you need something from the store? I've got to pick up a few odds and ends."

Mom has been smiling at me, and now she switches her gaze to Gran. "I have everything I need," she says. "You'll be back for dinner, won't you?"

"Heavens, no," Gran says. "Don't you dare fix anything extra for me. But thanks for asking. Didn't I tell you? Skylar's class sounds so interesting that I've joined a book discussion group at the library, and the first meeting is tonight. I'm looking forward to it."

"Oh, that sounds like so much fun," Mom says.

"Come with me!" Gran says enthusiastically. But she and I know what the answer will be.

"I can't," Mom says. "I'm swamped with work. I'd never be able to keep up with the rest of you."

I need to escape from this conversation, so I head toward the hall door, and Ben, seeing me leaving, yells, "Ben DOWN DOWN DOWN!"

I release the little slave driver from his chair and he follows me out of the kitchen. Morgan joins us in the hall, and he jumps over the gate while I'm still struggling with the stiff latch.

"Other one sis," Ben declares impatiently as I let him through the lower gate. "Yes? No? Yes?"

I carry him to the top gate and plop him down on the other side while I open the latch. He runs toward Alexandra's room, Morgan loping behind him. *Other one sis.* I like his name for Alexandra.

I'm not sorry to have him in the room with me this time. I don't want to discuss the priest with her anyway. Thank goodness she's never been particularly curious about Father Carrington. Once she said that she would never discuss her thoughts with anybody, but that's Alexandra. She's as independent as Morgan.

But what does she write in her journal then, if not her thoughts?

I stop my brother kicking on her door, and open it. "We're here," I say as the three of us enter.

Alexandra looks up from her journal. "I couldn't help hearing you. Where Ben goes is never a secret. Has he been eating his crayons again? He's got red stuff on his teeth."

"What next?" I say as I drag Ben out of the room and down the hall to the bathroom. He's not cooperative. He doesn't mind colored teeth, but he does mind his toothbrush. The cat wants no part of this scrubbing and spitting, and he vanishes with a delicate twitch of his tail.

Mom hears Ben's shrieks and comes upstairs to supervise the cleaning job. "You did that once," she tells me. "But you used green." She's smiling.

In class on Thursday, Mrs. Vargas tells us she's going to read another story. This one is called "There Will Come Soft Rains." The author is Ray Bradbury, and two of the kids have heard of him. I haven't, but I do my best to look intelligent. Tasha pretends to open an umbrella and even Mrs. Vargas laughs.

The story isn't funny. In a future time, an empty modern house filled with fantastic equipment runs itself. Outside, there are silhouettes of family members on a blackened wall. It's obvious that the last war is over and everyone has died. While Mrs. Vargas reads, I wonder what the discussion afterward will be like. What is there to say except that war is wrong? That's the only note I make, but I see the others writing rapidly in their notebooks.

At the end, Mrs. Vargas puts the book down. "Well, class, what do you think about this? Why do you suppose Bradbury wrote the story?"

We shift in our chairs and exchange stealthy glances. One girl raises her hand, and when she stands, she says, "This is some kind of warning. We aren't supposed to have wars."

Mrs. Vargas nods. "It's obvious from the way that the author describes the city that this war brought complete devastation. But . . ."

Mr. Parker is muttering audibly, impatiently, "No, no, no." I turn and see that he has his hand in the air.

"Mr. Parker?" Mrs. Vargas says.

He leaps up. "The story doesn't say that everybody is dead. There could be people still alive somewhere else." He sounds as if he needs to believe that this is true, that someone would even want to survive.

More hands go up. Other people agree with him.

I look around, baffled by them. Everybody in the world was dead. Can't they see that? There was no one left, no one left to struggle, to suffer, to try and then fail, try and then fail. At the end, even the wonderful house was gone.

Naomi DeAngelo stands and says, "It would be terrible, being left alive after something like that, because you'd feel so bad about the people who died. Maybe it would be better to die right away, with the others."

Mrs. Vargas calls on Mr. Sherman, the boy with the tattoo. "No, it would be better to survive," he says.

I try not to stare at him. Today his tattoo looks like a short strand of ivy. It can't be real. He is as silly as his opinion. I turn away, annoyed by him and his idea of the pleasures of survival. He has no idea what he's talking about.

"But you'd always feel bad," Naomi offers. "Wouldn't you? Wouldn't you care about all the people who died, maybe even members of your own family?"

I'm not going to listen to this. I'm going to walk out right now and go home. I start to get to my feet, but Tasha and that stupid Sherman boy glance over at me, so I sit back down.

"Did you want to add something, Miss Deacon?" Mrs. Vargas asks.

Oh, I could add plenty! But I shake my head.

She goes on to someone else, but I'm too angry to pay attention. I want this class to be over, and I don't care if the building bursts into flame to end it. I don't care if the world flies apart! Then they'd find out what it's like to be left behind!

I can't get my breath.

I look out the window, and in the old building across the street Alexandra stands in a window looking back at me.

No, it's not her. How could it be her? There's an art school on that floor of the building. I can see the sign clearly. The girl is much older than my sister, and her hair, pulled back tightly, is dark. She wears a pink shirt, though.

Alexandra likes pink and she wears it most of the time. I like pink, too, but that time I asked Mom if I could have the pink sweater at Nordstrom, Alexandra said, "Copycat!" and I chose the yellow one instead.

I almost hated my sister that day.

The bell rings and everybody bolts for the door, leaving me behind. I see Tasha and Naomi going out together, and a third girl, Miss Green, runs to catch up with them, laughing. I'm left behind with that idiot Sherman boy, who is grinning at me as if he knows me.

"Did you like the story today?" he asks.

"No," I say. We're passing Mrs. Vargas but I don't think she heard me. I don't want to hurt her feelings, but it was a really stupid story, the discussion afterward didn't make sense, and I don't want to write about it tonight.

"What was wrong with it?" the boy asks.

He seems determined to walk downstairs with me. I move farther away from him. Below on the stairs, I see the two girls I wanted for friends, with the third girl. They're chattering away as if they've known one other for a long lifetime. They've forgotten all about me.

"Well, what was wrong with it?" the boy persists.

"What's wrong with your neck?" I ask crossly.

I'm never rude! What's happening to me?

He fingers the ivy on his neck. "My sister does these," he says. "With colored ink. On the way to school." His face is so red that I hate myself. "She goes to the art institute across the street and she practices design on me every morning on the bus."

I blink at him foolishly. "I'm sorry," I blurt.

He shrugs and turns away from me, leaving me in the main hall by myself. I've hurt his feelings.

I hate this school.

In Alexandra's room, I tell her about the girls I thought might be my friends. "They ran off without even saying good-bye," I tell her. I know that I sound as if I'm about to cry, and I'm embarrassed. I want my sister to say, "They're mean. Don't you care one bit. You'll find better friends."

But instead she says, "I tried to warn you, Skylar. I wish you'd listen."

"You said I needed friends," I say.

"Then be more careful," she says. "Look what happened to you today. You trusted those girls and they let you down."

Something is wrong with this conversation, but I can't sort it out. It's easier to believe that I've been let down than to think through what has happened. It's always easier to believe what Alexandra says.

Ben is rooting through Alexandra's closet, throwing things out as he goes. I grab him with one arm and shove everything back with my right foot. Ben screams bloody murder. I shut the closet just as Mom opens the bedroom door.

"Skylar, I wish you wouldn't let him in here," she says. "He always makes such a mess."

"I'm sorry, Mom." I hand Ben over to her. He shuts up immediately and gives me an accusing glare.

Mom waits at the door until I pass her before she closes it carefully, softly.

I spend most of the afternoon trying to write a short paper about the discussion we had in class today. I could tell the truth and say that surviving a nuclear war is the worst thing that could happen to people, so maybe we'd all better hope that we die in the first few seconds. But instead, I end up writing that no matter how many amazing things humans invent, we're still stuck with our own bad judgment about how we use and misuse them.

I reread my paper twice before I take it downstairs to the computer. But I'm halfway through typing before I realize that my paper is probably just what Mrs. Vargas wants to see. She's the sort of person who expects people to take responsibility and march on. If I'd told the truth—*my* truth—she would think I was crazy.

Maybe, next Wednesday, I should tell Father Carrington how what seems true to me would actually seem crazy to everybody else. Probably I would never have to see him again. He'd dance around singing, "She's finally got it! She's crazy!"

Is that what it takes? Just admitting I'm crazy? Am I like someone who has stolen money and won't be punished so much if she admits that she did it?

After dinner, while I'm flipping through TV channels, Dad comes in and says he has a gift for me. He hands me a new cell phone.

"This is better than your grandmother's or mine," he says. "And it's much smaller, too. It will fit in your pocket."

I hold it, bewildered. "It's cute," I say finally.

"Cute," he says, and he laughs. "Well, I guess that's one way to describe it. It's all charged up and ready to go. Here's the instruction book, but I warn you, it's hard to read. If you've got time, I'll explain it to you now."

I'm still looking at the phone. "But why do I need this?" I say. "I don't have anyone to call."

The silence lasts a tick too long. I told the truth. I don't have anyone to call anymore.

Then he says, "It's to use in case you want to call home. You know, if it starts to rain and you want a ride." He pauses—and I let him suffer through the pause. Now I understand what he's up to. "You can use it if you decide to go to the library and want to let Mom know," he finishes.

"Maybe I'll call Gran while I'm riding the bus and tell her about the other passengers," I say, trying to go along with him——and not let him discover that I've caught him at his game. "Some of them are weird, and Gran always likes to hear about weird people."

Wrong thing to say.

"What weird people?" Dad asks quickly.

"Weird people like the old woman this morning who had her cat in a tote bag," I say, just as quickly. "The cat was meowing and the driver asked her what that noise was, and she said it was her sinus trouble echoing in her head."

Dad laughs unwillingly, then sobers. "You aren't being bothered by anyone, are you?"

"*Dad!*" I cry. "I'm not being *bothered* by anybody! If I ever am, I'll use the cell phone and call the police and you and even God, if His line isn't busy!"

Ben, who has been pulling a quacking yellow plastic duck behind him, stops and says, "No yelling."

I sigh, look back down at the phone again, and say, "Thanks, Dad. I'll feel better having this. In case it rains or I want to go to the library. Or if I just want to call home and talk for a while."

The last was what he wanted to hear. He smiles and pats my shoulder awkwardly. "Good," he says.

He picks up Ben and hugs him. Dad and I agree that I should test the phone, so I go outside to the deck and call our number. Dad answers and then puts Ben on the line.

"Gran?" yells Ben.

"No, it's Skylar," I say.

"Sy?" yells Ben. "Sy? Sy?" He'll go on yelling my name until Dad takes the phone away from him.

I turn off the phone and sit down on one of the deck chairs. Five crows are sitting in the apple tree facing me. One makes an odd sound, like a chuckle. The others lean forward as if they are about to take off, but then they settle back, ruffling their feathers irritably.

"What do you want?" I ask.

They flap away, cawing. After they're gone, a pair of sparrows perch on the edge of the birdbath and watch me. I sit still, barely breathing, and one of the sparrows bathes quickly, ducking his head under the water and then straightening up, so that beaded water floods down his back.

Ben bursts out the screen door, yelling, and the sparrows dart away.

"You're a pain," I tell him, and pull him to my lap. "You're a big pain, do you know that?"

He reaches for my phone and I slip it into my jeans pocket. "Nope," I say.

For once, he doesn't argue.

I bring the phone to Alexandra's room before I go to bed. "Look at this," I say. "Dad gave it to me."

"Good," she says. "Don't be embarrassed to use it if you have to."

I wish she hadn't said that. I don't need to be reminded. Now, standing here, I remember all the reasons I was afraid to ride the bus. Or to go to summer school.

Or to be alone in the house. Or to sleep in a dark room. Or to wake up in the morning. Or to survive. Or to wait.

chapter

FIVE

On Friday, Mrs. Vargas reads one of our papers and the class discusses it enthusiastically. Some people talk more than others. Tasha, Naomi, and Mr. Sherman speak as if they've been in this class for weeks, not days. I wish I could be like that, but I don't have anything to say that anyone would care about.

"I don't agree with what Mr. Sherman just said," Tasha is saying. "He isn't thinking about all the survivors who wouldn't know how to build things or grow their own food. How are they supposed to manage?"

Mrs. Vargas calls on Mr. Sherman to defend himself. "Then they'll have to do what their leaders tell them to do," he says. He has plenty of ideas about what the leaders should make everybody do. He's pretty bossy for somebody who let his sister draw a small yellow daisy on his neck this morning.

Mr. Parker hoots and says, "Yeah, King D.J. Sherman." He didn't raise his hand before he spoke, and Mrs. Vargas frowns.

D.J. Maybe the initials stand for Dumb Jerk. I can see him ordering survivors around. Build this! Plant that!

Mrs. Vargas reads another paper, and the red-haired girl slumps in her seat. The paper must be hers. She wrote that God wouldn't allow anything that horrible to happen so there's no point in worrying about it.

"Bad things happen all the time," Mr. Parker says. "God doesn't pay any attention." Tasha nods firmly.

Several students enter that argument. I draw daisies on my notebook cover until I realize what I'm doing, and then I scribble over them and draw Alexandra's suncatcher instead.

These kids are all so stupid. They talk about things they can't begin to understand. The biggest problem survivors would have is their own *thinking*. Their memories. Their dreams. They would never stop wondering if they could have changed the outcome. One word, or an act, or a gesture might have turned everything around before it was too late. But no. Ordinary people can't stop wars. Ordinary people can't stop some bad things from happening.

Mrs. Vargas reads a paper explaining how women could fix everything after a big war. The writer says that women were the ones who invented farming and preserving food, so they'd know best what to do.

Tasha is sitting very straight and looking out the window.

"What are men supposed to do then?" Mr. Parker asks irritably.

"The same things they always do," Tasha snaps at him. "Hit people and find a way to make booze."

Everyone in class bursts out laughing, even Mrs. Vargas. But she says, "Please raise your hand if you want to talk, people."

The bell rings. Class is over already? I look down at my desk and fuss with my notebook and pencil, stalling for time. I don't want to leave the room with everyone else and be ignored. I'll ignore them first.

"Let's buy doughnuts and eat on the lawn today," Tasha says to me. "Remember, we said we'd do it sometime." She's standing in front of me, smiling, one hand on her hip.

Naomi and the girl with dimples hear her and move closer. Tasha sees them and says, "Why don't all four of us go?"

Part of me wants to refuse, but part of me wants to go. Can I trust them?

"Sure," I say. "I love doughnuts."

I leave the room with them, a little breathless, my heart beating too fast. The other three talk at the same time, and I don't think they're listening to one another. I hurry to keep up with Miss Green.

"I'm Margaret," she says as we follow the other two down the stairs. "What's your name?"

"Skylar," I say.

Tasha looks back over her shoulder. "I love it. It sounds like something from a book."

My smile hurts my face, as if it didn't quite fit.

We're halfway across the street, heading toward the grocery store, when I remember the cell phone in my pocket. I have to call home and tell Mom, but what will these girls think if they hear me asking for permission? Nobody else had to do that.

But if I don't call . . .

"I have to call my grandmother," I say as I pull out the cell phone. "She . . . I . . ." I stop talking. The other girls are looking at me.

"Look at the cute cell phone!" Naomi says. "I want one like that. Mom gave me her old one, but I hate it because it's so heavy, so I never use it."

"You want to call before we go inside?" Tasha asks. "Hurry up, then."

They stand there, waiting.

"Go on inside," I say. "I'll catch up with you in half a sec."

They leave, and I call Gran's house, hoping she's there. She picks up instead of her answering machine.

"Some girls asked me to stay after class with them and I'd really like to," I babble. "I don't want to call Mom. I just can't do it. Will you tell her? Could you say her line was busy so I called you instead?"

"I was heading over there in a few minutes," Gran says. "I'll tell her when I get there. Have fun with your friends."

I shut off the phone and walk slowly toward the automatic doors. Friends? Doesn't Gran remember? I hardly know them.

I stop. They don't know anything about surviving. They're babies. And they won't like me when they get to know me.

"Hey, are you going to stand out here all day?" Margaret asks. She's waiting on the other side of the open doors. "Come on. Tasha and Naomi are buying up all the jelly doughnuts. If you want some, you'd better hurry."

I go with her, doing my best to smile and look as if I'm expecting to have a good time. What will Alexandra think about all this when I tell her?

We buy two big sacks of doughnuts and four cans of cold pop, then cross the street back to the school and sit under one of the trees. The grass under me feels damp, and the shade here is so cool that I shiver a little.

"I'm not supposed to eat anything that tastes good," Tasha tells us. "My dentist and my mother have decided that I'm much happier if I eat wood chips." She bites into a jelly doughnut and says, "Mmmm."

I open my pop can and reach for a doughnut after everyone else has taken one.

"I don't suppose anybody has napkins," Naomi says.

"Wipe your mouth on the underside of your shirt hem," Margaret advises us. "Who cares? We won't tell."

Jelly oozes out of my doughnut and lands on my pale blue T-shirt. "Too late," I say, and suddenly I'm giggling and can't quit.

"God, you're a mess," Tasha says, laughing her wonderful big laugh. "Here's some tissue."

"Lick it off your shirt," Margaret says. "It's quicker."

If I were home, I'd probably lick the jelly off and hope Mom didn't see me doing it. But I can't do that here. I dab at the jelly with Tasha's tissue, and now bits of tissue are sticking to my shirt, too.

"Give it back when you're done," Tasha says, snickering. "I might need it."

"Look who's got food." D.J. Sherman and Mr. Parker are standing over us, grinning and looking hopeful.

Do they see my shirt? I turn a little, hoping to hide myself, and I wish they would go away.

"Should we let them sit down?" Naomi asks.

Margaret and I shrug, but Tasha tells them, "Go buy your own doughnuts. You can sit with us when you get back."

The boys lope off, and Naomi asks, "What's with D.J.'s tattoos? Every day they look different. Is he using those fake tattoos?"

"They're designs his sister draws on his neck with ink every morning on the way to school," I say. "She goes to the art institute across the street."

"Hey," Tasha says, looking at me with great interest. "Do you know him?"

"Not really. He told me that yesterday."

"He's cute," she says. "He looks like he'd be lots of fun, but he's too short."

"I bet every boy you know is too short," Margaret says. "But I still wish I looked like you."

I finish my doughnut while they talk. They live in different parts of Seattle but they're becoming friends. Was I ever like that? Did I ever just assume that people would probably like me and not hurt me or whisper about me? Or leave me all alone?

The boys are back, with pop and another bag of doughnuts. They sit down, D.J. between Margaret and me, and Mr. Parker between Naomi and Tasha.

"What's your name?" Tasha asks Mr. Parker.

"Mr. Parker," he says. Then he laughs and says, "I'm Shawn."

Tasha tells the boys our first names, pointing at each of us as she does. D.J. nudges me with his elbow and says, "You're supposed to wear a bib when you eat jelly doughnuts."

What's wrong with me that I can't even eat without making a spectacle of myself? There's one advantage to not having any friends. You can't embarrass yourself in front of them.

"Let's do something together," D.J. says. "It's warm today. How about walking around Green Lake?"

My mouth is full. Without speaking, I begin shaking my head no, no, no. This must not happen. I can't go there.

D.J. notices and says, "Don't you like it there? How about going to the zoo then?"

I still can't swallow, but Tasha sees my problem and says, "Hey, she's trying to swallow. Give her a chance. I won't be able to go anywhere, though. My sister and I have to paint the back fence today or else."

"We'll all come over and help you paint it," Shawn says. "We'll have a paint party."

"Not a chance," she says. "I can tell by looking at you that Olivia and I would do all the painting and you guys would sit on the patio and enjoy the scene."

"We'll read you short stories," D.J. says.

"Hey," Tasha says, looking interested now. "You could read *Tom Sawyer*. That would be fun. But my mother will kill you. She warned me about letting anybody hang around, because it will slow things down."

"You're missing a good deal," D.J. says. He looks at me then. "You want to do something?"

I've finally swallowed, and I say, "I can't today. I have to baby-sit my brother this afternoon." The lie came so easily to me that I'm surprised.

I think about getting to my feet, telling everybody good-bye, and then walking across the street to the bus stop. But maybe a bus won't come for a long time, and I'll look stupid standing there alone in the glare of the midday sun. Stupid and exposed.

How am I supposed to solve this?

The other kids finish all the doughnuts. We sit in a circle for a while, talking about class, and then D.J. jumps up and says, "Okay, if nobody wants to do anything, I'll take off. See you guys Monday."

He throws the empty sacks and cans into the trash barrel he passes on his way to the intersection. He crosses, going north. We're watching him, but he doesn't seem to know or care. Could I be like that, so confident and relaxed?

The rest of us get up. "Come on, Skylar," Naomi says. "The bus stop's getting crowded. A bus must be due pretty soon."

She and I wave good-bye to the others and cross the street. The bus arrives immediately, and we're at the end of the line, so we have to stand.

"They're fun, aren't they?" Naomi says.

I think she means the passengers, and I look around, bewildered.

She laughs. "No, not them. I mean the kids from class. I had a good time back there."

"So did I," I say.

It's true, in a way. When I wasn't worrying about having a good time, I actually had one. I listen to her chatter all the way downtown and wave good-bye when we get off. Maybe I should call home and tell Mom that I'm on my way. But maybe I'd better not. There's no way of knowing how the conversation will go, and the last thing I want is an argument with my mother on a cell phone while I'm waiting at a bus stop with strangers.

Maybe the girls will ask me to join them again on Monday. Maybe the boys will be with them. We might get pastry again. Or go some-where else.

No! I shouldn't do that. I remember D.J.'s wanting to go to Green Lake, which is only six blocks from my house, and I know that I can't go there, not alone and not with anyone else. But what if they bring it up again? What would I say? I can't think of an excuse that doesn't sound stupid. They'd ask me too many questions. All of them talk so much and so easily—that's obvious from class. But talking gets people like me into trouble.

Sitting with them on the lawn was a really bad idea. Alexandra warned me, but I didn't listen to her. She'll have plenty to laugh at now, if I tell her. I spoiled everything. I could have had casual friends—just a few. But I went too far. I was trying to pretend that I was like everybody else.

Gran meets me at the front door. "All clear," she says.

We join Mom and Ben on the back deck. Ben has stacked most of his books in a pile, with the obvious intention of trapping somebody into reading to him for hours. Both of them look up at me, but Ben says, "Read, read, read!" to Mom.

"Did you have a nice time?" Mom asks me, and she sounds inter-ested. I can see that she's working hard to be fair to me. Gran must have performed real magic here.

"Sure," I say. "I spoiled my lunch with doughnuts and pop, though. We ate on the school lawn."

"Who's 'we'?" Mom asks, a little too eagerly.

"A big bunch of us from class," I say as I sit down and drop my notebook to the floor. "Tasha, Naomi, Margaret, D.J., and Shawn."

Mom smiles. Her relief is irritating. Did she think I was going to eat with babies or old men? No, she's just remembering Alexandra, who befriends anybody.

Why am I dwelling on that now? I don't have to make trouble for myself. I don't have to poison myself with my own thoughts, Father Carrington says. I can choose to think something different.

After a while, Gran leaves to run errands and I volunteer to read to Ben for a while. Mom takes advantage of this to go to the den and E-mail a cake recipe to my aunt. Ben grabs the hem of my shorts and says, "Other one sis, okay?"

"Not now," I say. "I thought you wanted somebody to read to you."

"Nope, nope," he says. "Other one sis, okay?"

I don't want to talk to Alexandra. She'll ask questions, just like Mom did, and I don't want to go through the whole thing all over again. And I don't need nagging.

"I'll push you on the swing for a while," I tell Ben.

"High?" he asks, holding one hand over his head.

"No," I say. "I have to keep you safe."

chapter
SIX

What's the point in anything? What's the point in cleaning my room and putting away my clean laundry? What's the point of taking a shower and washing my hair? Why don't I just sit here on my bed until the world comes to an end and nothing matters and nobody matters and we all spin off into darkness?

If the world ends tonight, I'll tell God, *What the hell were You thinking about when You did what You did! Is this whole thing a joke to You?*

I asked Father Carrington once—*that priest!*—if he thought God might be female, and he said, "Why not?"

"What kind of answer is *that?*" I asked.

"What kind of *question* was that?" he countered. "You sound like your grandmother."

"She thinks God is female," I said.

"I know she does," he said. I expected him to sigh, but he didn't.

What would the kids in class think if they knew I wondered about God's gender? They'd laugh. No, they might not. Tasha wouldn't.

She's smart and curious, and she has a good sense of humor, but she doesn't make fun of people.

I put away the clean clothes stacked on my bed, shower and wash my hair, blow it dry, and then I go to bed with the book I've been reading.

I wake up past midnight, the book open on my chest, and my bedside lamp on. Alexandra is standing in my doorway.

"I can't talk to you now," I say quietly. "It's too late. I don't want to wake anyone." I dread the conversation we'll have sooner or later about my staying after school.

She turns her back on me and leaves without another word.

Down the hall, Ben shouts, "Drink! Ben wanna drink!" He sleeps in the small alcove off my parents' bedroom instead of in the bedroom that overlooks the backyard, the one Gran has been decorating since he was born. He plays in the room—it's full of toys—but his crib is in the alcove, so Mom doesn't have to go so far in the middle of the night to check and make sure he's still breathing. At least, that's what Gran says. I think Mom keeps Ben there to make sure nobody steals him and leaves us waiting again.

I hear Mom moving around, murmuring to Ben. Ben wants something to eat, too, but Mom says, "No," firmly.

I close my book and turn out my light, then stare at the ceiling. We can't always let people do what they want, but where do we draw lines?

❦

In the morning, I hear the rain before I'm fully awake. Rain on a Saturday. What fun. I roll over and slide back into sleep.

I finish dressing shortly after eleven and head for the stairs to check out the sound of Dad's power screwdriver. I've been hearing it for fifteen minutes.

I find him at the head of the stairs, installing the tallest gate I've ever seen. "Where did you get that?" I ask. "It's enormous."

"I've got two of them," Dad says. "A fellow from the office brought them over this morning. He used them to keep his Great Dane in the family room before he had doors installed. I think we can keep Ben where he belongs now."

The gates are metal mesh, with sturdy hinges. I need both hands to work the fasteners that close them. "Keep your screwdriver in the trunk of your car," I advise Dad. "Ben's getting to be pretty handy around the house."

"Sy, Sy, Sy!" Ben shouts from the kitchen, so I follow the racket. He's in the high chair, flinging bits of animal crackers around the room. Morgan is batting one of them across the floor, and his tail is bushed out. When we do battle with elephants, we need to look tough.

Mom, busy with the coffeemaker, looks over at me and says, "I wanted to take Ben to the zoo today."

"It's not raining too hard for that," I say. I take a handful of Ben's animal crackers out of his bowl and sit down at the table. "You've got the rain cover for his stroller. One of the kids wanted to go to the zoo yesterday, but——"

"Oh, you couldn't do that." Mom stops what she's doing to stare at me, shocked. "You hardly know them. Sharing snacks at school might be all right, but you couldn't—"

"They're nice!" I argue, although I still don't trust them completely myself.

Why am I doing this? I can't win. The truth is that part of me doesn't even want to win! But I've begun a journey. Haven't I?

"They're really nice," I say. "I know you'd like them if you met them."

"People can seem nice," Mom says slowly. She plugs in the coffee maker and fusses with the dishcloth, carefully not looking at me. "People can seem safe, but we can't always tell."

She's right, of course, but I can't agree with her, because I'm afraid she's going down a road I don't want to follow. Now that I'm in summer school, I don't want to quit. I can stick this out if I just keep my head. Then the English course will be out of the way and I can take the costume design class in the fall, and then I can do things for the drama class productions, and maybe even have a life. Well, part of a life.

A brilliant idea presents itself to me. "If you're not going to the zoo, maybe you can take me to the library," I say. "I'd like to check out some short story books. Mrs. Vargas got me interested in them."

Mom is all smiles, now that I've shown her how much I need her. "What a great idea!" she says. "While you're doing that, Ben and I can spend some time in the children's section."

The library is less than a mile away, and Alexandra and I used to walk there. But that was in the good old days, when rain hardly ever fell in summer and everybody had friends.

We have lunch early, Dad takes his car to the garage for tinkering, and Mom drives Ben and me to the library in her car. I find three short story collections, dawdle for a while in the poetry section, and then check out a book about Elizabethan clothing. I can hear Ben yelling and laughing now—it's time for us to leave before the librarians ask us to go.

On the way home, we stop at the grocery store. By the time we reach the house, Ben is ready for a nap. A short one. I struggle through the barricades on the stairs going up, get Ben's green blanket out of his crib, and then repeat the task going down. Ben grabs his blanket and drags it to the family room.

"Read!" he shouts, holding up one of his new books to show me.

"Skylar's got her own books," Mom tells him. "I'll read to you."

Rescued. I take on the lower gate at the stairs again, climb halfway up, and stop. I should tell Alexandra we're back.

Well, she must *know* that already, I tell myself. We've been making enough noise.

Part of me is looking for an excuse to talk to her. Part of me dreads it. Yesterday I should have done what I do every day after school. I should have stopped by her room to tell her what happened. I'll have to face her sooner or later, so I might as well do it now.

I open her bedroom door. She's sitting in the window seat, watching raindrops slide down the glass.

"We're back from the library," I say. I know I sound nervous—and guilty.

"I could tell," she says, and she turns halfway, almost facing me but not meeting my gaze.

"I checked out a lot of short stories," I say. "I like them better than

I used to. And I found a book with great drawings of the clothes people wore when Elizabeth the First was queen."

Alexandra traces raindrops on the window and she watches her hand, not me. "You were late getting home from class yesterday."

"I stayed after with some of the kids," I say.

She doesn't respond, so I fill in the silence with babbling. "We had doughnuts and pop, and we ate on the lawn. It wasn't as warm as I thought it would be—"

"Did you tell them about me?" she interrupts.

"Of course not!" I cry, shocked. "No! Why would I do that?"

Alexandra shrugs. "Well, now that you've got all these new best friends, I thought you might want to tell them everything."

"No. I'm not telling anybody anything."

"You'll end up telling," she says, and she sounds bitter. "You've always told things that you shouldn't. You talk too much." She turns to look at me now, her hair swinging. She's so cold! So judgmental!

"What's wrong with you?" I ask, so hurt that I'm ready to cry. "Why are you acting like this?"

"I warned you not to talk to people so much. You can't trust anybody. Why don't you listen, Skylar? You have no idea what you're getting into."

"You wanted me to make friends! It was your idea!"

"You can't blame me for anything," she says. "You brought this all on yourself. I can't believe how stupid you are sometimes."

"I can't believe how stupid *you* are!" I cry. She's turned on me! She's hurt me so much that I don't think I can survive this. "Don't you dare blame anything on me. I'd still have friends if it weren't for you. Everything that's happened is because of you, Alexandra. All this is *your* fault! Why were you so careless? You couldn't run—you just got your ankle out of the cast. You couldn't get away—"

Alexandra turns her back on me and looks out at the rain. "Be quiet," she says. Her voice is dead and flat. "Just get out of here and leave me alone."

I go, gladly, and I slam the door behind me. Anger feels so good now. I *want* to be furious! I want to shout and throw things and—be *alive!*

It *was* all her fault!

I close my bedroom door behind me and burst into tears. I shouldn't have quarreled with her. It *wasn't* her fault. It might even have been mine. I need her and I shouldn't have argued with her. I don't know what to do or how to fix this.

I could go to her room and apologize, but if I do that, then I'll be right back where I started. She's afraid I'll talk too much and she doesn't want me to be too involved with anyone else. I *won't* talk too much. I'll be careful—and I'll still have friends. Sort of. Perhaps they'll only be acquaintances, but I'll have something to be glad about.

Alexandra wants me to be happy. Of course she does!

I lie facedown on my bed, wishing I could die or disappear or be transported to the other side of the world where no one knows me. Where Alexandra can't find me.

I like church best on the Sundays when not many people come. The rain stopped late last night and the sun is bright and hot today, so only a third of the pews are filled. People have gone off boating or swimming. Gran planned to spend the day across the Sound, so I don't expect to see her.

Father Carrington likes days like this, too. I can tell, because he takes a little longer with the liturgy, savoring the words. Everything is calm and lovely until communion, and then Ben begins singing with the choir, only he is singing the purple dinosaur song and the choir is singing my favorite hymn, "Jesu, Joy of Man's Desiring."

"Make him stop," I hiss to Mom. But how can she, short of clapping her hand over his mouth?

Dad and I get up to take communion, but Mom stays behind with the Beast. While we're in line, I hear the purple dinosaur song drowning out "Jesu" and I'm so embarrassed I could die.

When my turn comes, I kneel at the altar rail and Father Carrington holds out the host to me, murmuring, "Skylar, this is the body of Christ."

My throat tightens suddenly. I sob once, hard and uncontrollably, and cover my face with my hands.

There is silence, but it isn't cold and hostile. It's like an embrace. I look up and Father Carrington looks down into my eyes. I hold up my hands for the wafer and put it in my mouth. He moves on, sober.

The chalice bearer moves one step toward me, but I shake my head. I don't like to drink the wine, and Father Carrington told me that I don't have to do it.

I can't get up. Dad helps me to my feet. The woman standing behind me, waiting for her turn to kneel, smiles and reaches out to touch me. I try to smile, too, but my mouth is trembling too much. This is a disaster. I've done exactly what I never wanted to do, make a scene.

Ben, unaware of anything but his own pleasure in being alive, shouts, "Looky!" He's holding Mom's prayer book upside down. "Da cow jumpt ober da MOON!" he yells.

The people sitting around us stare and a few smile. One woman scowls. Mom says, "Hush!" to Ben. Dad says, "Benjamin," in that warning voice Ben ought to heed but never does.

Ben should be in the nursery. I'm not coming to church again unless Mom promises to leave him in there with the rest of the little kids. My brother is a pest, and even worse, he causes people to notice us.

But then, so do I. Who ever heard of anyone starting to cry at communion?

Everything bad is beginning to happen all over again. We're a spectacle. We'll have to leave this church, too, sooner or later. We're the crazy Deacons, yelling and bawling and looking demented.

On the way home in the car, I tell Mom that she must leave Ben in the nursery next Sunday. I don't soften my words or apologize for my irritation. I want to settle this—to solve the problem and move on. I want to control something for once.

"He's too little for the nursery," Mom says flatly.

"There are kids younger than he is, in there," I say. "He'd like it. They play games and have lots of fun."

"I won't leave him with strangers," she says. "I will never do that."

"The women in the nursery aren't going to do anything to him!" I say. "There's nothing wrong with them."

"I won't leave him there," she says. "That's final, Skylar."

"Then I'm not going back to church," I say. "I'm tired of being embarrassed by him. He doesn't mind us and he bothers everybody."

Ben, secure in his car seat, smiles fondly at me. "Here," he says, and he hands me his ratty old teddy bear. "Kiss Boo Bear and make you well."

I begin crying. I'm hopeless and helpless, and my brother shames me with his innocence and goodness.

"I'm sorry, Mom," I say, but it's too late. We've crossed a line that I didn't know was there until it was too late.

Ben goes down for a nap in my parents' room when we get home, and Mom lies down, too. Clouds sweep in and cover the sun. When I hear thunder, I leave the deck for the house, taking my book with me. Moments later, rain lashes the backyard, heavy sheets of it. The violence of the storm astonishes me. Is this God, commenting on my behavior in church?

On the way I treated my mother on the way home?

Mom is up, and she's crying in the living room. "I can't bear not knowing," she says over and over. Dad pats her shoulder helplessly. "I know," he says. "I know."

Through the kitchen window, I see Alexandra walking in the backyard, along the edge of the lawn where the pink carnations bloom among the white roses. Rain drenches her. Her dress clings to her. Her hair is sopping and stringy. By the time I reach the deck, she is gone, leaving me with the wreckage.

chapter
SEVEN

Monday morning, I go downstairs to find Gran in the kitchen, fixing breakfast as if it's something she does every day. Mom didn't get up, but Gran doesn't say anything except that she's in the mood for waffles and thought she'd share with us. Ben approves enthusiastically and bangs on his high chair tray with his wooden dog.

I take my place at the table. "Morning, everybody," I say.

"Sy!" Ben yells.

Dad smiles a little at me. He looks tired and ill, and when Gran puts his plate down in front of him, I see him straighten up, as if eating waffles is something like facing execution. Waffles used to be our favorite breakfast, even the frozen ones like Gran brought over this morning.

"Hungry!" roars my brother, and he pounds on his high chair to make certain Gran's listening.

"He's already had a waffle," Gran tells me as she takes another tray out of the oven. "He ate half of it and threw the other half at the cat."

"Morgan likes waffles," I say. Gran gives me two and I pour raspberry syrup over them. "Yum. Thanks, Gran."

"It's still raining," Gran says as she looks out the window. "What awful weather for June."

She isn't going to offer me a ride, is she? Any other time I'd hope for one, but not now, not when I'm handling the bus and school better than anyone thought I could. Including me.

"I'll bring my umbrella," I say briskly, without looking up, hoping that this simple solution will put the problem to rest. Dad pays no attention and helps himself to another waffle. Gran only nods.

The conversation changes to Ben's table manners, which grow worse instead of better. For a while he tried to eat with a spoon, but lately he's been using his fingers again. Right now he doesn't care about our opinions and he continues painting the front of his pajamas with a finger dipped in orange juice. "Whoa!" he exclaims, admiring his work.

After his second helping of waffles, Dad leaves for his office. I have plenty of time to change my T-shirt for a sweatshirt and shove my notebook in my old backpack, along with my umbrella.

When I leave, Gran and Ben wave good-bye from the front window. The silent sleepers in the house still dream, while the rest of us get on with our day.

Halfway to the bus stop, two crows sheltering in a maple tree caw at me through the downpour. On the other side of the street, another sits boldly on someone's covered deck and hurls its own insults at me. I don't understand why these birds threaten me. Perhaps they feel threatened by me. But I don't throw rocks at them and I do my best to ignore them. Am I invading what they think is their territory? Does the neighborhood now belong to them?

Until this moment I felt free and glad to be away from the house.

For an instant, I'm tempted to return home and crawl back in bed. If I could sleep for a very long time, maybe everything would go away.

No. I'll turn this day into a success. I won't be too friendly at school, and I won't be unfriendly. I'll be careful about what I say. I won't talk too much.

A few black crows in the rain can't mean bad luck.

Mrs. Vargas reads D. H. Lawrence's poem "Snake." When she's done, she says, "Do you think poets watch themselves as well as others? Is Lawrence saying that there was a time when he was told things that turned out to be wrong, or is he asking us to look at ourselves? Have we believed when we should have questioned instead?"

I draw Alexandra's suncatcher.

In the morning, when I look in the mirror, who am I seeing? Not myself. Someone is there, someone who appeared without warning, and this pale lie of a girl believes that she is as real as everybody else.

That is not true. I dig my pencil into the paper. Everything I see *is* real.

At lunch, in a place near school that serves great hamburgers, I catch myself saying, "I don't mind baby-sitting my brother exactly, but he's always getting into things. He's so fast! It only takes him a second to disappear—"

I stop suddenly. Alexandra drifts past the window behind Tasha and she glances once at me, warningly.

"My little sister put her doll blanket in the oven and Mom turned the oven to preheat without looking inside first," Naomi says. She waves a french fry, emphasizing her words. "All the fire alarms went off at once. We could smell the smoke in the house for days."

"Was she playing 'laundry room'?" Margaret asks. "Mom says I did that once. I put my pajamas in the dishwasher and my quilt in the oven, but she caught me in time."

D.J. pushes his plate toward me. "You didn't order fries, Skylar. Do you want some of mine?"

"Thanks, but I like salad better," I say. That should be brief enough to satisfy Alexandra. But maybe she would rather that I just said, "No thanks."

Shawn reaches for D.J.'s fries, but D.J. slaps his hand. Tasha gives Shawn five or six of hers.

"You have a sister, too, don't you?" Tasha asks me. "Is it easier for her to take care of your brother?"

I remember how much Ben loves Alexandra. Well, why shouldn't he? After all, she's never the one who's stuck with the job of cleaning him up when he wants to stay grubby or running after him when he doesn't want to be caught. His other one sis doesn't baby-sit, but I can't tell them that, so I simply say, "He has more respect for her."

"How old is she?" Tasha asks.

I open my mouth to say "Fifteen," and shut it again. How old is Alexandra? I can't remember. How long has it been? How long? *How long?* I am saturated with panic. I see my hands shaking and I put them in my lap. I've got to say something, but what?

". . . and my sister and her friend poured bubble bath into the john and flushed it. You wouldn't believe the mess I had to clean up!"

Naomi has been talking. Did anyone notice that I didn't answer Tasha's question? But they're looking at Naomi, not me.

"Are we having dessert?" D.J. demands. "Or are we going out into the storm while we're still hungry?"

"We're having dessert," Shawn says. "Where's our waitress?"

The waitress comes and we order. I'm not hungry. I want to go home to stop myself from saying something foolish while there's still time, but I don't want to leave because, in spite of the danger, I'm really having fun. I like these kids. We suit each other. But I must be cautious or I'll ruin everything.

We all order the same thing, hot fudge sundaes. A small squabble begins when the waitress brings them and one has two cherries on top. The waitress, shaking her head, resolves the problem by taking away one of the cherries.

"She's carrying away any hope for a tip, along with that cherry," Shawn complains.

"We'll give her extra money to make up for you being so selfish and greedy," Naomi says calmly, digging into her hot fudge.

Finally we can't stall any longer. We've finished and it's time to leave. I called Gran before I came here and promised to call again when I left, but I don't want to do it in front of the others. I'll call at the bus stop. But Naomi will be riding downtown with me. I'll have to wait until after she transfers to her other bus.

Everyone walks with us, even though I'm the only one with an umbrella. The bus comes soon, too soon, and I catch myself smiling when I wave good-bye.

"That was lots of fun," Naomi says as we find a seat together in the back.

"Maybe we can do it again sometime," I say.

No, it's better if I never do anything like this again. After all, we'll only be together for the summer, and once we go back to our regular schools, we won't stay in touch anyway. But it's been such fun!

"Do you have far to walk after you get off your next bus?" she asks.

"A few blocks," I say. "I don't mind."

I consider telling her about the crows. There was a time when I wouldn't have hesitated talking about them because they've taken such an interest in me. But I remember that I shouldn't talk so much, so I ask Naomi if she has pets and let her talk the rest of the way about her two dogs and cat and about the stray puppy she's been trying to catch for a week. She's still telling me about animals when we get off at the transfer point.

Her bus comes first, so as soon as she's gone, I use my cell phone to call Gran at my house and tell her I'm on my way. "How's Mom?" I ask.

"She's fine," she says, and I know she's lying.

"How could you do something so irresponsible?" Mom weeps as soon as she sees me come in the house. "How could you go off with strangers? I've been frightened out of my wits."

"I called Gran and told her I was having lunch with my friends," I say, trying to stay calm. "These are the same kids I told you about, Mom."

"You don't really know those people!" Mom cries. "You just met them. What are they doing in summer school? I don't understand. Did they fail the class when they took it before?"

I see Gran signaling me with her eyebrows, but I don't understand the message, so I have no choice but to struggle on.

"Tasha is taking the class because she wants an extra music class in the fall," I say, trying hard to sound reasonable and calm. "Naomi and Margaret want to finish high school early so they can enter college early, too. Shawn transferred from another state and there was some problem with his transcript. D.J. wants to go to art school with his sister and—"

Horrified, I see Mom yank at her own hair, weeping. "How can you worry me like this? I can't bear to worry and not know. I can't bear waiting."

"I called Gran!" I say in a louder voice. Mom's not listening. I don't know what to do to help her because I don't know what she wants to hear.

Ben struggles loose from her. "No cranky," he says. "No, no."

Mom reaches for him again but he runs toward the stairs and begins crying. He sounds frightened.

Gran takes Mom by the arm to stop her from following Ben. "Nora, I insist that you sit down now," she says. "I insist. I'll fix you a cup of tea."

Mom blinks. Now she looks like a small child. "I'm sorry, Cass," she tells Gran. "I'm so sorry. I don't know what's wrong with me."

"It's no matter," Gran says. "Come on. Rest in the family room while I heat the water."

I start after Ben, expecting to find him trying to open the new gate at the foot of the stairs. I reach it at the same moment I see him climbing the gate at the top. "Hey, hey!" he shouts triumphantly. He's so fast!

I struggle to open the lower gate, but the fastener is stiff. The gate is too tall for me to step over, and I doubt if the mesh would hold my weight if I try to climb it the way Ben did. I've broken a fingernail below the quick and it hurts. At last, I get it open, run up the steps, and then I have to struggle with another fastener. This is maddening!

"Ben!" I call out, trying to sound calm and cheerful in case Mom hears me.

At last the gate is open. I run down the hall to Alexandra's room. The door is closed. I open it and the room is empty! They're gone!

She's taken him! She's left with him, and she can barely walk, even with her cane. How can she take care of him and protect him when she can't even protect herself?

What am I going to do?

Stop it! I tell myself. She hasn't left the house with him. No one passed me on the stairs, so they've got to be up here somewhere.

I go to my room next, but it's empty. So are the other two bedrooms and the small bathroom off the master bedroom. Finally I open the main bathroom door, and there is Ben. He's climbed up on the counter and he's running the cold water over his feet.

"What do you think you're doing?" I ask him furiously. "Look at you!"

"Foots are wet," he announces, pleased. He reaches for a toothbrush.

"Everything about you is wet," I say as I pick him up and take away the toothbrush. "Why don't you use the bathroom like everybody else does. I mean *use* it, not play in it."

"Okay," Ben says cheerfully.

I hug him and hate myself for yelling. Does Mom feel this way about him, too? He's so exasperating—and so completely perfect.

I change Ben's clothes, getting absolutely no help from him in this project, and then we return to Alexandra's room. He wants to walk by himself, but I want to carry him and feel him safe against me. My Ben, my helpless little brother, who is trying to grow up in this house filled with tears and shadows.

Alexandra is there now, sitting in the window and silhouetted against the rain. She's writing in her journal again and she doesn't look up.

"I thought you were gone," I say. "I was afraid you had left." I don't tell her that I was afraid she had taken our brother with her.

Alexandra still doesn't look up. "You don't need me," she says coldly. "You have all your new friends, those people you talk and talk to, those people who will whisper about you as soon as they find out who you really are."

"Up," Ben says. He's smiling at Alexandra and reaching out to her.

"I love you, Ben," Alexandra says, returning his smile. But she doesn't smile at me—or even speak to me.

"What about me?" I say. I try to sound cheerful, but it doesn't come off, and I sound like a spoiled brat instead. Or maybe a scared little girl who wants to change the subject.

Silent, Alexandra looks back at her journal, and her pen moves gracefully across the page. I know that her handwriting is prettier than mine, artistic and fine, like everything about her. I would be like her if I could, but I can't. I'm not all the things she is and has been. I'm only Skylar.

I carry Ben out of her room and close the door.

What does Alexandra write in that journal? I wonder. Day after day she writes in it, as if it were more important than anything else she's ever done. I won't spy on her and read it when she's not there, but I can't help wishing I knew what she finds to record. Does she write about me?

Ben and I go downstairs. He yawns and rubs his eyes, and Gran, seeing him, takes him and says, "Time for a nap already?"

"No nap," Ben says and yawns again.

"Yep," Gran says.

The family room curtains are closed and Mom is sleeping on the couch. I can hear the rain on the windows and I love that sound. Gran tucks Ben in at the other end of the couch and drapes the fuzzy afghan over him. She sits on the floor beside him for a few moments, rubbing his back. With one last small protest, he falls asleep. Morgan leaps up next to him, purring, his eyes half-closed with pleasure.

Gran makes hot chocolate for me in the kitchen and we sit down together. "Did you have a good time at lunch?" she asks. She really sounds interested, not worried. She sounds as if she expects me to enjoy myself.

"Yes, I had a great time," I say. I taste my hot chocolate, savoring the richness that always makes me think of velvet, and then I take a big swallow, stalling. I'm not sure what kind of time I had anymore. Alexandra's words changed what I thought was fun to something else. I probably looked and sounded ridiculous at lunch.

"I trust your judgment about people," Gran says. She's not looking at me, so I know she doesn't trust my judgment completely. "But you could give her the benefit of the doubt sometimes, all things considered."

We're back to that again. All things considered, I'm lucky I'm not handcuffed to my mother.

"What about Ben?" I ask. "What's going to happen to him? He's not going to be a two-year-old baby forever. What happens when it's time for him to start kindergarten? Or does he have to stay home with Mom for the rest of his life?"

Gran blinks and sighs. "Well, things are bound to get better."

"It's been nearly three years," I say.

Now I remember! Now I remember how old my sister is. She's eighteen. It's been three years since she was fifteen. Since she was my age.

I stand, still holding my cup. I've got to get out of this room before I say something I shouldn't. Gran and I don't discuss Alexandra.

"I'd better start my homework," I tell Gran. "The teacher read poetry to us today, and it's not always easy coming up with something to say after you've talked things to death in class."

Gran nods and I leave the kitchen. I have absolutely nothing to say about the poems we heard today. Too much has happened since then.

After Dad comes home, Gran fixes spaghetti for dinner, and Mom comes to the table. She seems perfectly all right. Her nap did her good. Her eyes are clear and she's changed clothes, wearing a blue cotton skirt that's too big for her now and a white shirt. Ben appreciates the new atmosphere and celebrates it by mashing his green beans into paste and offering samples to everyone.

I eat quickly and leave the table, pleading that I still haven't finished my homework. Actually, I haven't even started it. Of everything that happened today, what is the most important? A homework assignment or sorting through the terrible truths that emerged later on?

Alexandra is angry with me. But I only did what she said she wanted me to do. I made new friends.

What does she really want from me? I'm afraid to ask.

Is there a short story about sisters like us? Or would it take a book to tell the tale? How could it possibly end?

chapter
EIGHT

The morning sky is gray and heavy, and I hurry toward the bus stop, hunched inside my summer jacket. The wind is thin and mean. I remember once when Alexandra and I were on our way to our piano lessons and a cold rainstorm began suddenly. That was in June, too, but neither of us wore a jacket that day. My music books were safe in my backpack, but Alexandra hated backpacks and carried everything in a flowered cloth tote bag that Gran had brought back from Paris. We ran, laughing like idiots, until we reached the studio. Then Alexandra found that the music books in her bag were wet and the pages were stuck together. I stopped using a backpack last year or maybe the year before, after finally taking Alexandra's advice seriously. It was all right to look different because, after all, I was different. But today I look like everybody else on the way to summer school, because I *am* like everybody else.

Three blocks from my house, I step off a curb to cross an intersection and a car whips past me—but not too fast for me to see two girls I once knew, sitting in the backseat.

I hesitate and lose my balance. For a moment, I'm afraid my knees will give way. I know that Kris and Joanie saw me. Their pale faces were turned toward me, their mouths open in surprise. Their mother did not slow down or stop for me. What did Kris say to me the last time I called? "My mother doesn't think I should talk to you anymore." She sounded like a stranger, distant and quiet. I said good-bye, but she had already hung up and I spoke to a dead line.

I am frozen here in the street. I can't move forward or back to the curb. The gray sky whirls over me and the street tilts under my feet.

A crow flaps close to my face, a quick black warning. Startled, I catch control of myself and struggle across the intersection, forcing my legs to walk, gasping for every breath. The crows are waiting for me on the other side, perched on a fence, their heads turning first one way and then the other as they study me curiously. One, perhaps the one who saved me, mutters something that sounds like a query. "Grrrrk?" he asks.

"Oh, god," I say aloud. I'm shaking. Tears spurt from my eyes. Without the crow, I would be lying in the intersection, helpless with a tired old grief, worn out with losses I can't remember because there are so many. I don't know whether to thank him or throw a rock at him. Does he know that another car might have come and ended my dreams of swans? And ended my waiting?

I should return home, but I'm still crying, and I can't deal with my mother at a time like this. When I reach the bus stop, an elderly man wearing a baseball cap looks at me, glances away, and then looks back and says, "Help you, missy?"

I shake my head. I don't have a tissue, so I am reduced to turning my back and wiping my nose on my sleeve. The old man taps my shoulder and hands me a new packet of tissues.

"Summer colds are the worst," he says when I thank him, and then he acts as if he has a great interest in the bus stop sign, to let me sort myself out in privacy.

When the bus comes, he gets on first, pretending that he doesn't see me. I'm grateful for this last kindness, too.

Why was it easy for him to help me—and impossible for the friends I had? But wait, wait. In the end, didn't he look away, too? Pretend he didn't see me? The gesture was kind in him and terrible in my old friends. What is the difference? What don't I see here? Is it that the suffering of a stranger can be dealt with, but the suffering of a friend cannot be borne? And then, did they hate me in the end because they had hurt me while I was already hurting so much?

Tasha and Naomi are waiting for me outside the school, sitting together on the steps. They stand up when they see me.

"D.J.'s sister drew on his face instead of his neck this morning," Tasha says, grinning.

"He looks like he's wearing a tiger mask," Naomi said. "Wait until you see him. He's gorgeous."

"Naomi's in love," Tasha says, nudging the girl with her bony elbow.

"It's hopeless," Naomi said. "He likes Skylar better. Anyway, I have a boyfriend. Sort of."

"Sort of? What's his last name?" Tasha asks. "Sort of *what*? Sort of Smith?"

"Sort of Krakowsky," Naomi says. Her giggle reminds me of Ben's, the kind of happy sound that invites others to join in.

I shake my head, laughing at them. The security guard smiles his chilly smile at us as we pass him. The main hall is full of kids, and someone is whistling. Feet clatter on the stairs.

I'm relieved to be here, safe from old friends who became enemies. As I climb the stairs with Tasha and Naomi, I remember lunch the day before. Maybe we can do that again. Maybe we'll do other things together, lots of things, and when I go home afterward, I won't tell Alexandra. She doesn't need to know everything I do.

Oh yes, she does. I can't hide from her.

D.J. is facing the door when I enter the classroom. He does look like a tiger. His sister has painted stripes on his face in such a way that he is transformed. This is no cartoon tiger and no child's toy. This is *Tiger*, regal and calm.

I shake my head and take my seat. D.J. is the center of attention. Even Mrs. Vargas moves close to see his wonderful face.

Naomi slides into the seat next to me. "He's so cute," she whispers.

I pretend to scowl at her.

"So what's going on?" she whispers. "You didn't say you already had a boyfriend."

"I don't," I say.

"Then?" she says. "Then?"

"Then nothing," I say.

She goes back to her own seat. Jenny McMichaels, the girl who has the place next to me, sits down. We don't talk much. She's shy but

I've seen her talking to a couple of the other girls. I look around the class and, for the first time, I realize that the kids have formed small groups of friends. It's been happening all along, but it didn't register on me until now. What draws us to certain people? I'm sure this brown-haired girl next to me is nice enough, but Tasha and Naomi are my friends. And Margaret, too, with her dimples. What is this magical thing? Gran once said that we are chemically attracted to some people and not to others, but that doesn't make sense. No, there are vibrations that certain people give off, and we like them. We make a kind of unsung harmony with them. We sing "Jesu" with them.

Tasha squats down next to my seat. "Listen," she says.

I interrupt. "Do you know 'Jesu, Joy of Man's Desiring'?" I ask.

"Bach? You're talking about Bach?" she asks, bewildered.

I nod.

"Of course," she says. "I've got a piano transcription of it, and we sing it at church."

I'm so relieved that she knows what I'm talking about. I wish I had the courage to hug her, but she would think I'd lost my mind. Knowing a hymn isn't such a big thing.

"Okay, what did you want?" I ask her, but it's too late. Mrs. Vargas is tapping her pencil on her desk, so Tasha goes back to her seat.

"She could be a model," Jenny says wistfully, looking after her.

I'd thought that Tasha could be a professional musician, because she has what Gran calls "presence." She's more than just good-looking. She's enthusiastic about things, and so she takes charge, both in class and at lunch. Jenny sees one thing in my friend and I see another.

"She's funny, too," I tell Jenny.

"It helps," she says. She sounds sad. Is it because Tasha doesn't single her out for friendship? Why does Tasha single out me? And Naomi and Margaret, too?

Halfway through class, I see Alexandra watching me through the smudged window in the door. What is she doing here, spying on me? Checking to see if I talk too much? But then her blond hair swirls and she is gone.

Oh, if only she truly were gone!

No, I don't mean that! I'm sorry, Alexandra. I didn't mean it. I need you. And what would Ben do without his other one sis?

Mrs. Vargas is talking about pronouns and I am drawing swans on the inside of my folder, where no one can see them. Or catch them. Or keep them from coming home to us.

I bend over my desk to crush my half-born sob.

After class, Tasha says, "Let's go to a different place for lunch today. Do you like fish and chips?"

"I know a place," Margaret begins.

"Everybody knows a place," Shawn says. "The question is how long has the fish been out of the water?"

"Oh, you're a winner," D. J. says disgustedly. "Don't you know better than to gross people out when they're talking about food?"

"It's cold outside," Naomi says. "Why don't we have chili?"

I shake my head. "I have to baby-sit my brother," I lie.

"We'll come to your house, then," D.J. says. "We'll stop on the way and get takeout." The tiger smiles at me.

I shake my head again. "Ben's not feeling very well. He won't take a nap if you guys are there, and Mom would kill me."

"We can't have you getting killed," Shawn says.

I gasp. Tasha looks sharply at me, and I see something in her eyes. Bits and pieces coming together. A knowing. Or was it already there?

"I'd better go," I say, and I hurry away, leaving them standing near the top of the second-floor stairs.

Now they're talking about me. Now they're comparing notes. Now I'm losing them.

I don't need friends. If I give them up, Alexandra will be happy. She warned me about letting people get too close. She knew it might come to this. Why didn't I listen to her?

A bus is sliding to a stop in front of the grocery store. I run to catch it and climb on a split second before the door hisses shut. I find a window seat and stare blindly out. How many weeks of summer school left? Too many. We pass dingy buildings and shabby storefronts on our way downtown. It's such an ugly world.

I have to be truthful with myself. Everything was better before I decided to take this English class. Mom was happy because I wasn't riding the bus and having lunch with strangers. Dad was happy because I wasn't frightening Mom. Alexandra was happy because I wasn't talking too much.

Well, nobody was really *happy*. What a laugh. How could we be happy? But at least we weren't totally, completely devastated every single living moment.

I want Alexandra. I want God to give me my sister and not play games with me anymore. But what does God want in exchange? Isn't there always a deal somewhere? Somebody wants something and has to give up something else, right? The sacrifice has to be important, doesn't it? Oh, God, You don't fool me. You want the big things. You want firstborns. You even wanted Your own firstborn. You don't kid around with sacrifice.

Okay, I'm ready, God. What do You want from me? What do I have to give You in order for You to do what's right?

The bus is half full. There aren't many kids, and they aren't the kind I'd want to know. The man sitting in front of me turns to look at me for a moment too long. I glare at him. He grins, and I see that his front teeth are broken. I look out the window again, and when I think he's facing the front, I glance at him.

He's staring at me.

I recoil and he laughs. "Hey, babe," he asks. "How are ya?"

I look out the window.

"Babe, I'm talking to you!" he shouts.

I ignore him.

"I'm talking to you!" he yells.

"Leave me alone!" I yell back.

I look toward the driver for help, but I see him watching me coldly in his rearview mirror as if this is *my* fault. I get up and move, and the man moves, too, sitting next to me. He smells awful.

See what you get? Alexandra asks.

"Who do you think you are?" the man demands. "Just who the hell do you think you are?"

The gray-haired woman sitting in front of him turns in her seat and says, "Leave the child alone! What's wrong with you? Do you want to be dragged off to jail?"

"By you and what army?" the man yells. "Mind your own business."

We've reached my transfer place and the bus stops. The man puts his foot up on the back of the woman's seat and won't let me pass. The woman shakes her head and gets off, leaving me standing there. "You'll end up in jail someday," she tells the man disgustedly.

I'm only worth half a battle? She's deserting me?

"I have to get off," I say loudly but I don't make eye contact with him. I want someone to intervene, help me. Save me.

"You have to do what I tell you to do," the man says.

Oh god, oh god, I don't know what to do. The bus will start again and I'll miss my transfer and . . .

Alexandra drifts down the aisle, smiling a terrible smile at the man. I pull out my cell phone and say, "I'm calling the police."

The man leaps away from me as if I'd struck him. "I'll fix you," he says, and he gets off the bus.

"Come on," Alexandra says. "We'll call Mom and have her pick us up."

I follow her off the bus, looking around for the man, but I don't see him.

"Call Mom right now," Alexandra urges. "Tell her this isn't working. Tell her you made a mistake. You're not ready to go anywhere by yourself."

"But you wanted me to go to summer school," I say feebly.

"Are you all right, honey?" a short, dumpy woman says. "Are you okay?"

I stare at her, clear my throat, and say, "Yes, thank you."

"You look like you're ready to faint," she says. "You look like you've seen a ghost."

I'm holding the cell phone and feeling like an idiot. My transfer bus pulls up and I find myself getting on automatically, still holding the phone.

"You take care, honey!" the woman calls after me.

I look around for the man, but he's not on the bus. I sink into a seat just as my knees give out.

Alexandra didn't get on with me.

What does she want me to do? I don't understand her anymore. She wanted me to have new friends, and then when I found some, she didn't like it. She wanted me to go to summer school, and now she doesn't.

What does she want? What does God want?

I lean my head against the window. Okay, okay. There's a bargain in here somewhere. I just have to find it. Until I do, I'll give up friends. There's a sacrifice for You, God. Just let me know what else You want.

I'm sure You will.

When I get off the bus, I call my house, just to tell Mom I'm practically there. I listen while the phone rings, planning what I'll say. Do you need something from the store? I can say. Just thought I'd call and ask.

She doesn't answer, and after a while the answering machine picks up. Dad's voice says only, "Please leave a message." Nothing else. I end the call without speaking. She must be there. She would never let me come back to an empty house.

I hurry, watching for cars and crows and dirty men. I hold the phone in my hand, ready to call for help. At home, I find Mom sleeping with Ben on the family room couch. Ben sits up as soon as I walk in the room.

"Sy!" he yells happily.

Mom doesn't stir. She sleeps with her arms covering her head. I call her name but she doesn't answer. She breathes lightly, quickly, as if even in her dreams she's frightened.

I call Gran first and then Dad, using the phone next to the couch. By the time they reach the house, Mom is awake and sitting groggily with Ben on her lap.

Morgan stares at me from the back of the couch.

Gran comes in first, but before I have a chance to explain anything, Dad comes in, too, gray-faced.

"What have you done?" Mom asks me. "Why did you call them?"

I tattle. "She was sleeping so hard," I say. "I couldn't wake her, and I was afraid she was unconscious. Ben was here and . . ."

"Why are you acting like this, Skylar?" Mom asks. "I don't understand you anymore."

Neither do I. I haven't understood me for a long time. I go upstairs to Alexandra, to let them sort it out for themselves.

Alexandra, writing in her journal, looks up. "Your jacket isn't warm enough for a day like this," she says. "Why don't you use my pink one? It's just right."

She sounds like her old self. She isn't angry with me anymore. Relieved, I sit on the edge of her bed. "You know Mom would hate it if I borrowed anything of yours."

"She wouldn't know the difference," my sister says. She goes back to her journal. Her long hair hides her face.

I watch her write and I'm feeling peaceful again. Maybe I'll ask Mom to take me to school tomorrow. Maybe I won't go at all. I could drop out. What difference would it make?

Maybe, if I don't have friends, I can have Alexandra and she will keep me safe. What happened on the bus could have been a sign.

"Was what happened on the bus a sign?" I ask her.

She pushes her hair back and smiles at me. "What do you think?" she asks.

chapter

NINE

"A sign?" Father Carrington asks. His eyebrows rise. "A sign from God? A man with broken teeth hits on you on the bus, and you ask me if this is a sign that you're supposed to give up summer school? It's a sign that the man belongs in a zoo!"

The willow tree thrashes its branches. Sunlight glitters. I stir in my seat. "Well, you don't have to have a cow over it," I say. "I was just asking. People talk about looking for signs from God all the time. The Bible is full of signs."

"Your life is not full of signs," he says. "You have not been given a warning to either sacrifice school or suffer the consequences. You should have gone to class today. The next time somebody treats you that way on a bus, stand up and scream. That will get the driver's attention. That will get you plenty of attention from everybody, and the jerk will probably jump through a window to get away from you."

"Maybe it's not the right time for me to be doing things . . ." I begin.

"No. We're not going over that again. We're talking about school now. You should have gone. It's bad for your mother and bad for you when you hide at home. What are you going to do tomorrow?"

The tree is almost still. A leaf here and there trembles a bit, waiting for my decision. What am I going to do? Mom was happy today when I said I was staying home. I told her I had a sore throat, and she was *happy*. What's wrong with this picture?

"I'll go back to school," I say, and a faint hope lights one corner of my world. Tasha, Naomi, and Margaret will be there. We'll go somewhere after class and I'll forget all this for a little while.

Alexandra stands behind a veil of willow branches, watching me. I close my eyes for a moment, and when I open them again, she's gone.

". . . on the bus, too," Father Carrington says. He writes something on a piece of paper. Perhaps it's a contract between the two of us. *Skylar promises to go to school on the bus. Amen.*

"On the bus," I agree, and a thrill of fear dances down my spine.

"Have lunch with your friends tomorrow," he says, still writing.

"Maybe *they* won't want to have lunch with *me*," I say.

He looks up. "You can ask, Skylar," he says. He sounds exasperated. Should he talk to me that way? He's starting to sound like a parent.

I shrug, making a show of pretending that I don't care, and I give the tree more attention. A yellow and gray bird is there. I've never seen one like it before.

"A goldfinch!" Father Carrington says. "That's the second time I've seen one. Do you suppose it has a nest around here? We seldom see them anymore."

The bird flicks its wings and leaves.

Father Carrington sighs. I can tell that the bird is more interesting than I am. Perhaps it takes the bus to school and phones all its friends every night to talk about clothes.

"Let's get back to that bus ride," he says, sounding businesslike and brisk.

"I don't want to talk about it anymore," I say.

"Because you think Alexandra was there with you," he says shrewdly. "That's why you don't want to talk about it anymore. On the bus, you finally remembered that you had a cell phone for emergencies and scared the creep off with it, but you don't want to take credit for helping yourself, so you're giving it to Alexandra instead." Somewhere in the rectory a phone rings, but the phone on his desk is silent.

I am silent, too, waiting for the yellow bird to return. When it doesn't, and when That Priest doesn't say anything else, I sigh and say, "How do you know that she *wasn't* there?"

I hear a quick rap on the door. Father Carrington gets up and shuffles across the carpet. He opens the door a crack and says, "Yes?"

A woman's voice says something I can't quite hear, but I can make out the word *hospital*.

"Tell them I'm coming," he says. He closes the door and comes back to his desk. "A parishioner has been injured in a car crash," he says. "I have to go to the hospital. I'm sorry. Do you want to come back tomorrow so we can finish our conversation? I think we should."

I get to my feet. "I'll see you next Wednesday," I say. "I'll wait for Gran outside."

"God is *not* testing you," he says. "This is not a game. He wants you back in the daylight again, not hiding in the shadows."

"How do you know?" I ask, and I walk out.

He follows me to the front door and opens it for me. I see dazzling sunlight and an empty parking lot edged on two sides with dark shrubs where anything could be hiding. I can't go out there, where I'll be exposed and vulnerable. Alone. Or worse, not alone.

"Wait in here," he says, when he notices my hesitation. "You can watch for your grandmother from the window."

Somewhere I find anger and the desire to contradict him. "I'll wait outside by the door," I croak.

"Not with Alexandra!" he says. "Not with your sister. She can't help you."

But our argument ends when Gran's car pulls into the parking lot. I run out to it without saying good-bye.

As if I could summon Alexandra whenever I wanted! Give *me* a break, priest.

Gran drops me off and I find Mom making cookies in the kitchen with Ben. She smiled all morning and she's still smiling.

"I hope you're in the mood for cookies and juice," she says. "Ben's already had his share."

"Sy!" Ben yells, and he bangs on his high chair tray with his plastic cup. It wasn't empty, so now he has orange juice in his hair.

I get the juice from the refrigerator and wonder why Mom never asks me how things go when I'm with Father Carrington. She has never asked me, not even once. How long will I have to be counseled by him before she's curious? I could smile and say, "Well, we talked about signs from God today, and a dirty, smelly man who scared me on the bus." I won't because that would be a serious mistake, but part of me wants to see if she dares to take an interest in my real life.

"Is your throat better?" Mom asks as she hands me a plate with four cookies on it.

"It's fine now," I say.

"You'd better stay home tomorrow, just in case," she says. "Summer colds can turn into something serious."

"Yo!" Ben yells, and he throws part of a cookie at Morgan. Morgan sniffs the cookie contemptuously.

I'm saved from another argument about staying out of school because the phone rings. "Can you get that?" Mom asks.

I picked up the phone and hear, "Skylar! It's Tasha. What happened to you today?"

I sag against the counter, weak with surprise. And shock. From the corner of my eye, I see Mom watching and listening. She holds a spoon in one hand, caught in the middle of something, and neither of us can remember what it was anymore.

"I had a sore throat," I tell Tasha.

"How are you now?" she asks. "Are you coming to school tomorrow? We missed you."

"I'm better," I say cautiously. What am I supposed to do? Agree to go to school with my mother listening? I know she's forgotten the spoon that she's holding

"We had lunch at the hamburger place again yesterday, but I don't know where they went today. I had my music lesson, so I couldn't go with them. D.J. asked me twice if I had your phone number. I guess he hasn't heard about phone books yet. I had to call six Deacons before I found you, though. Maybe he's working his way down the list, too."

"Why would he do that?" I ask, pleased and uncomfortably aware that I'm blushing.

She laughs. "Beats me. Oh, come on, girl. Wake up. Hey, he's back to wearing a snake on his neck again, and we met his sister this morning. You'd love her. She showed us these dangly earrings she made herself."

"Great," I say weakly. "I wish I'd seen them."

"Mrs. Vargas is reading another story in class tomorrow," she says. "You don't want to miss it."

"Right," I say. "Right," I say again, louder. "I don't want to miss that. I'll be there."

"And we'll do something afterward," she says.

"Sounds good to me," I say.

After I hang up, I realize Mom has left the room. I hear her and Ben in the bathroom down the hall. She left the spoon on the counter.

I go to my bedroom before she can ask me who called and why. But then, maybe she wouldn't ask. Maybe she dreads hearing answers. Answers could be like pale light shed on her soul. Or like promises that might not be kept.

I go to school Thursday, after an argument with Mom. My anger keeps me from being afraid. I'm halfway to school before I realize that I didn't see the crows in the neighborhood. We hear a story in class, and afterward, my friends and I share doughnuts on the lawn again. I don't say much, and what I do say comes out in the form of questions, so that the others talk instead. D.J. waits at the bus stop with Naomi and me, soberly telling us about art school. No one accosts me on the way home, so altogether, it was a successful day. Alexandra didn't show up anywhere, but I didn't need her, either.

When I go to bed, it occurs to me that a day like this can be a trick.

On Friday, Jack Fisher, the boy who sleeps in class most of the time, gets up in the middle of class, groans, and collapses on the floor. The cap he always wears has fallen off and, shocked, I see that he is bald. Mrs. Vargas shoos us out of the room. A girl from class says, "Jack has leukemia."

Men come with a stretcher and equipment, and while we hover in the hall, we hear them murmuring. A radio crackles with static and distant harsh voices. The men leave with Jack, who is attached to tubes now. His face is gray and shiny.

I realize that Tasha and I are clutching Margaret's hands. "My brother died of leukemia," Margaret says.

Tasha hugs Margaret, and Naomi and I circle them with our arms. We are an island among the others, who stumble about and shake their heads. Mrs. Vargas comes and asks Tasha something, but I am running after my swan and I can't hear her.

Come back! Don't leave me here where people are still dying and nobody stops it.

Mrs. Vargas takes Margaret back into the room and closes the door. Tasha, Naomi, and I lean against each other. D.J. and Shawn seem to be helpless, patting us uselessly and saying, "Come on, let's go. Let's go."

Oh, God, look what You've done this time! You just can't get it right, can You? You give me a scrap of peace and then yank it back. Bully!

We got to the tearoom Gran pointed out on my first day at school. We sit at a corner table and Tasha takes charge of us in that paneled and carpeted room. I feel out of place, clumsy and ugly with my burning eyes and red nose.

"We'll have orange pekoe and brown toast, please," she says to the waitress.

"For everyone, Tasha?" the waitress asks.

"Is that all right, everybody?" Tasha asks. Her dark eyes are still swimming with tears.

We nod silently. After the waitress leaves, Naomi says, "You must have been here before. It's so . . . elegant." Her voice is so soft that it's almost a whisper.

"My mom owns it," Tasha says. "We won't get a check." Suddenly she starts laughing and crying at the same time.

"Aw, jeez," Shawn says. His voice cracks.

The waitress is back with cups, saucers, and napkins. "Tasha, are you all right?" she asks. "Do you want me to call your mother?"

"I'm okay," Tasha tells her. "Thanks, Milly."

We sit in a strange silence until the tea and toast come, then everyone cheers up at the same time. What is it about a small and quiet meal with friends that *fixes* things? Have I just discovered something important? Do kings and presidents know about this? An elaborate banquet can't repair anything, but simple food in a quiet place can turn bad things into the bearable.

"I've never been in a place like this before," D. J. says. He watches Tasha pour her tea through the strainer, and he does the same.

"The only reason they let you in is because you're with the owner's daughter," Shawn says, and he laughs, then looks around to see if laughter is all right with the rest of us. Must be. I don't see the laugh police coming, I think, and I catch myself grinning.

I look at my watch. I don't have to call Mom yet. Perhaps I can spend this time here and still make the usual bus, and she won't have to know anything. I can't imagine a conversation where I would tell her that a boy in my class might be dying.

Tasha sees me look at my watch. "You're okay," she says. "You've got plenty of time."

"For what?" D.J. asks.

"She has a hot date with somebody who's taller than you," Tasha says.

Now I feel as if sunlight had found me here. I risk glancing at the window, and I do not see my sister watching me. Not this time.

But then I remember our classmate who was taken away on a stretcher, and I know that God is still out there, clumsily harvesting. Breaking hearts.

I skip church on Sunday. That old "sore throat" is back. If I work this right, the sore throat will show up often enough to get me out of things I don't want to do but not so often that Mom drags me to the doctor.

I stay away from Alexandra's room until Sunday night. When I walk in, I see her leaning against the window. She looks sick.

I don't want to be here. But I must be here. "Are you all right?" I ask.

She opens her journal but she doesn't write in it. "I waited for you," she says tiredly. "I waited outside the tearoom for hours and hours."

"I was only there half an hour," I say.

"Hours," she says.

"I didn't talk much," I tell her hastily.

"I know."

She begins writing, so I leave her alone. Gladly.

Tasha calls me that night to tell me that she saw a girl from class who told her that Jack died. I hardly knew him, but I cry, and I hear her crying, too.

"I wonder if Margaret knows," I say.

"We should tell her," Tasha says. "We can't let her find out in class. Shall I do it?"

"Yes," I say. "You'll tell it right."

I know this is true.

When I hang up the phone, I look out the window. Twilight has fallen and there are no shadows except for my sister, who drifts along the fence, looking up into the sky where a single large bird flaps over our yard.

I've found a way to handle things. I have lunch with my friends every other day. I never talk much. I have a sore throat every other Sunday and every other Wednesday, until the middle of July, when the priest catches on.

"What do you think you're up to this time?" he asks me.

The climbing roses outside his window are bright red, but they aren't as good as last year's. We had too much rain in June.

"I'm not up to anything," I tell the willow tree.

"If you're having sore throats all the time, you need to see a doctor," he says. "If you're lying about it, you need to knock it off."

"That's no way for a priest to talk," I say. The tree raises a warning branch.

"What are you up to?" he asks again.

"Nothing! I told you before that I'm going to school on the bus every day and I've got friends. Isn't that what I'm supposed to be doing?" A rose releases its petals in disgust and sheds them on the clipped shrub under the window.

"What are they like, these friends of yours?" Father Carrington asks.

I'm tempted suddenly to tease him. Oh, they all have broken teeth and smell, I could say.

Instead, I say, "I told you before. They're nice. We have lunch a couple of times a week. One of them calls me up sometimes."

"Do you ever call her?" he asked.

I hesitate, then say, "A couple of times."

"Was your mother home when you did it? Did she overhear you?" The tree waits, not a leaf stirring.

I shake my head. "Of course not. Why start that up again? It would only upset her."

"You have to start it up again. It's bad for both of you, playing this game of hers." I can hear him tapping his pencil.

"What game?" I ask coldly, turning to look at him.

He sighs. "The 'Let's not let Skylar get hurt' game. You need your own life."

"I've got it," I say. "I have nice friends and I like my class, and nothing else bad has happened on the bus."

"And?" he asks.

I know what he wants. I won't give it to him.

"Is this some sort of deal you've worked out with your sister?" he demands. "You have friends—but barely—and you like your class—but not too much—and you carefully ride the bus."

I start to say something and then quit while I'm ahead. I watch the tree again.

"Or do you think you've made a bargain with God?" he asks.

I blink several times but don't speak.

"So you've started that," he says wearily. His chair creaks as he leans back in it. "Go ahead and try it, but be sure you understand that you'll never know more than your own side of the bargain."

"What's that supposed to mean?" I ask angrily.

"You'll understand when the time comes," he says.

I catch myself picking the thread out of the hem of my T-shirt. "I don't like you when you're not wearing your clerical clothes," I say.

He leans back in his chair again, looks at the ceiling, and says, "Give me a break."

Is he talking to God? Does he actually know God? Does anybody?

He straightens up suddenly and says, "Do you know what an anniversary is?"

"Of course I do," I say.

Then I understand what he means. After July comes August. How dare he do this to me!

"If I admit I'm crazy, would I still have to come back here?" I ask angrily.

"Where else can you go—you with the sister?" he says. "You and I are the only ones who know about her. You're stuck with me."

"Ben knows," I say.

I hear him suck in his breath.

"Don't involve him," he says. "It's cruel."

"He knows her," I say. "He sees her even when I'm not around."

Now *he's* the one who can't stop blinking. Serves him right.

chapter
TEN

I sit on the edge of my bed in the dark, wondering if anyone in Seattle is sleeping tonight. It's unbearably hot and my head aches. I argued for days to be allowed to open my window at night, but now that I've won, I doubt if it makes a difference. The dusty air hangs motionless, inside and out. My cotton nightgown sticks to me. My sheets are wrinkled and damp. I can hear the new air conditioner in my parents' room rumbling, and I do my best to crush my resentment, because Ben must have a cool place to sleep.

My window is high above the backyard, and no one could reach it without a ladder. Still, Mom is convinced that an army of men wait on the other side of the fence for the lights in our house to go out so they can haul their ladders into the yard, prop them against the wall, and overpower me. Sometimes I've wondered if perhaps there might actually be one or two men hiding with their ladders. My mother's fears, even now, are as contagious as the flu.

So, because of the heat, my window has been open for two nights. Mother comes in every hour to check on me. If I've been lucky enough to fall asleep, I jerk awake, mindless with fright, until she says, "It's only me." Last night I waited until she retreated to her cool and noisy cave to slip into Alexandra's room, looking for sympathy.

"I can't stand much more of this," I told her.

Alexandra, silhouetted against the glow from the streetlight, said, "Mom's not the only one worrying about that open window. I wish you'd keep it closed, too. You never know what might happen."

"Don't you think I'd hear someone putting a ladder up against the house!" I exclaimed. "This is ridiculous."

"But you're still worried about it, aren't you?" Alexandra said. "You can't fool me."

Obviously she didn't understand. I went back to bed.

Sometimes I wonder if Alexandra is taking our mother's side in everything now. I've even wondered if I can tell the difference between the two anymore. Whatever I do seems to upset both of them. There was a time when things were different.

Well, there was a time when everything was different, but we're never going back there again. I'm beginning to look at that head-on now, instead of glancing off to the side and hoping that the dark goes away before I find out what it's hiding. I can feel this happening, but I'm not ready to think it through yet. I don't really have to look at it tonight. Not yet.

August is coming.

I heard once of a brokenhearted girl who turned her face to the wall and just died. Where did she go? Somewhere cool, I hope. Somewhere cool where she could sleep in comfort forever, and never ever have to deal with anything bad, not even nightmares.

I hear Ben crying, even over the rattle and rumble of the air conditioner. He's got a bad rash on his chest and back, and the ointment the doctor gave Mom doesn't help much.

Morgan comes in, arches his back for a moment, and then jumps to the windowsill. He presses his forehead against the screen.

I gather up my pillows and lie down on the wooden floor. It's cooler here, but I'm too bony now to be comfortable on such a hard place. I go back to bed and find Morgan waiting there, purring.

"Do you love me, Morgan?" I ask softly.

Now he rubs his forehead against me.

What is the name of this lonely place where I live? Could I find the name in a book? Perhaps a book of myths? When Alexandra and I were little, Gran told us stories about fairies and dragons and kings, and at the end of each story, everything turned out all right. Bad people were punished and good people were happy. I wish we were little again.

What is the name of this lonely, terrible place? Who can rescue me?

At school, I find D.J. and Tasha sitting on the steps, where we always meet before class. "Where's everybody else?" I ask.

"Naomi and Margaret are doing something different with Margaret's hair," Tasha says. She gets to her feet slowly, as if she aches all over. "We haven't seen Shawn yet."

"What's wrong with you?" I ask Tasha.

"What's wrong with me is my father's crazy idea that we're going to fix up our whole house this summer," she says. "Last night we worked until midnight putting up paneling in the basement rec room, and he wants to paint the kitchen today. It's going to reach the high nineties again, but will I be at the beach? No."

D.J., wearing a ring of small, smiling, green turtles around his neck, says, "How about you, Skylar? Want to go swimming?"

"No," I say abruptly, and then I soften it, adding, "I've got stuff to do at home. Maybe some other time." I hope I haven't hurt him.

But he sighs and stretches, showing long, tan arms. "Maybe Shawn will."

Just before the first bell rings, Shawn jogs across the lawn and joins us. Halfway down the hall, the girls come out of the lavatory and show off Margaret's French braid.

"I like it," I tell her, and Alexandra, ahead of me on the stairs, turns to stare at me coldly.

I don't speak again.

Mrs. Vargas reads "First Confession," by Gran's favorite author, Frank O'Connor. I don't know the story, but I smile when Mrs. Vargas begins, her voice taking on a slight Irish lilt. The class settles down in comfort. All the windows in the old room are open. The sky outside is blazing blue.

The story is both funny and disturbing. A little boy complains about his truly mean sister and grandmother, and at the end, his priest comforts him in a way that causes the class to burst out laughing. The priest reminds me of Father Carrington, in a way.

When she's done, Mrs. Vargas puts the book down. "Well, what do you think? The story was long, so we won't have much time for discussion. Did the priest handle the boy's confession the right way, or did he add to the problem?"

Hands shoot up. Mrs. Vargas calls on Shawn, who says, "The priest did the right thing. But I wish somebody had punished the sister. She was the one who deserved it."

Tasha agrees. "The sister and the grandmother were awful."

But Margaret says, "The boy should have been punished more, because he threatened his sister with the bread knife. That was terrible. And he should have been made to forgive his sister for the things she did to him."

Another girl objects to this idea. "Forgive the sister? She was so nasty!"

Most of the class agrees with that.

"Sisters are always a pain," one girl says emphatically, and I hear Tasha laugh. Her sister Olivia drives her crazy.

My sister is different. Alexandra is never really mean to me. She only wants to protect me, and she would never treat me the way the sister in the story treated her brother. But yet, didn't Alexandra do something that was much worse?

Mrs. Vargas goes to the board and underlines tomorrow's assignment. August 1, 250 words on "First Confession."

I have spots before my eyes. August 1. Time rolls over me, crushes the breath out of me, murders me. August is almost here.

Alexandra touches my hand. "Class is over," she whispers.

I look up and Tasha smiles at me. "Daydreaming?" she asks.

I see the pity in her dark eyes, and I bite my lip savagely. I will not cry! We're the last ones out of the room, and we catch up with Margaret and Naomi halfway down the stairs. I wish we were having lunch together today, but Tasha must meet her father at the paint store and the boys are going water-skiing with Shawn's older brother.

After much discussion, Naomi decides to go home with Margaret to teach her how to braid her hair six different ways. I'm invited, but I decline.

I take the bus home with Alexandra, who sits beside me weeping. "What is this place?" she cries.

Gran takes Mom and Ben downtown to shop for toys and clothes in a big, air-conditioned department store.

"Please come with us," Mom says. "It will be so much cooler than the house, and if you stay here, you'll have to keep the doors closed and locked."

She's getting worse every day. "I have a lot of work to do," I say. "I've got a paper to write and I don't even know where to start." The last thing I want is an afternoon in a department store, no matter how cool it is.

Mom leaves me a jug of lemonade in the refrigerator, and I'm about to take it upstairs with me when the front doorbell rings.

I find Tasha on the porch. I gape at her.

"I thought you were painting something," I blurt, dumbfounded to find her at my house.

"I got fired," she says, doing her best to smile, but the effort must be too much because the smile disappears. "No, I'm lying. I told Dad I had an emergency. Would you like to go for a walk? Someplace where we can talk?"

I still can't understand why she's here. "Why? What's wrong, Tasha?"

"I think we need to talk about something," she says grimly. "I don't want to come in. I mean, your mother . . ."

"She's not here," I say. "My grandmother took Mom and Ben shopping."

"Then can I come in?" she asks. "Please?"

At the same instant I swing open the door, I realize that she doesn't ask if Alexandra is home. *She knows.*

Tasha comes in, looks around, and says, "What a pretty living room. If my parents had taste, this is what they'd have. Instead, we're stuck with the first thing they see in the furniture store windows."

"It's hot in here," I say nervously. "I was going upstairs, but it's probably even hotter up there. Let's go outside and sit in the shade. Mom left lemonade for me."

"Good," Tasha says. "Lead the way."

I'm shaking. My hands and my lower lip tremble. In another moment, my teeth will be chattering. What is she going to say to me? Morgan, seeing the possibility for a new friend, weaves through Tasha's legs, practically tripping her. Tasha scoops him up and cuddles him.

I put the lemonade jug, two glasses, and a plate of cookies on a tray and carry it outside. Tasha carries the cat. We sit uneasily side by side on the lawn swing, and then, suddenly, Tasha gets up and sits at my feet instead.

"I have to sit facing you," she says. "And I don't want to talk very loud because I don't want your neighbors to hear."

I nod stupidly, wishing the rest of the day could disappear in a flash and tomorrow would come instantly, relieving me of this burden.

"I know about your sister," she says.

Did I hear her right? Has the worst thing happened?

"How?" I ask. I pour lemonade and spill it. Tasha helps me.

"My mother is a volunteer for Mothers in Crisis," she says. "I was talking about you one day, and I said your last name, and she asked me if I was sure I had your name right. Skylar Deacon. She asked me if you'd had a sister named Alexandra, and I told you you did. She said the MC group helped your mother put up posters about Alexandra and they sent out flyers. You know, all the things people do . . ."

I nodded. I want her to go home right now. She has found me out.

Tasha puts her hand on my knee. "I'm really sorry. I'm so very sorry, Skylar. If I can ever do anything for you or your family, please tell me. My mother would do anything she can for you, too. She's helped lots of people."

"We have help," I said. I'm so full of resentment that I don't dare say anything else. Who knows what toads will pop out of my mouth? I don't want charity. I don't want people feeling sorry for me. I don't want pity, and I see it all over her face.

Tasha opens her mouth and shuts it again. She nods. "Sure," she says. "I only wanted you to know that—"

"What?" I want to punish her. I want her to say exactly what it is that she wants me to know. That she can fix things? That anybody can fix this? That someday I'll forget about it?

Her dark eyes fill with tears and she wipes them away on the backs of her hands. "Sometimes when I look at you, I think you are haunted. I don't mean in a bad way."

I don't speak, so she is left with the words in her mouth and nowhere to go. Haunted? Of course I'm haunted.

She sits back on the grass and covers her face with her hands. I've hurt her. I wanted to do it but now I'm ashamed of myself.

117

"It's very hard sometimes," I hear myself say. What a stupid remark. It's *always* hard.

I end up telling her about that day in August, three years ago. I listen while I talk, and I am amazed at what I can say without screaming or weeping. Alexandra, who had broken her ankle in January when she was thrown from a friend's horse, had needed surgery, and then she had worn a full leg cast for months, then a shorter cast, and finally, on that day . . . on *that* day, the doctor removed the cast. She was free. She had to use a cane, but she could walk anywhere she wanted.

Mom left us at home while she had her hair cut. Alexandra, restless and unable to sit still, said, "I'm going to walk down to the lake to feed the swans. Do you suppose they'll still remember me? I haven't been there for a long time."

"That's six blocks away," I said. "You'd better not go so far."

But she wouldn't listen. She tore up most of a loaf of bread and put the bits and pieces in a plastic bag. I remember that it was brown and white with the name of a bookstore on it. I was willing to go with her, but she wanted to go alone. Or maybe she just didn't want to keep me from what she knew I wanted to do, practice my new piano piece.

I didn't mind staying behind. Alexandra had a relationship with the swans that I didn't understand, and I was almost but not quite jealous. She would whistle the first three notes of "Clair de Lune," and they would skim over the water toward her. When they reached the shore, they lost their grace and struggled clumsily across the grass to her. Even so, they were beautiful, with white glistening wings, perfect feathers, and gleaming eyes. They loved her. Everyone loved her.

"They're earthbound," Alexandra told me once while I watched them waddle toward her. "They're meant to sail on the water or in the air. I wish I were a swan."

She had been earthbound for months, and on that August day she was ready to fly again. I watched her leave, leaning heavily on her cane, swinging the plastic bag in her free hand, her long pink dress fluttering around her ankles, almost but not quite hiding the hideous scar from the surgery.

Then she was gone.

Mom returned. I helped her make dinner, stuffed pork chops and squash. Dad came home a little late. We didn't eat but instead went to look for Alexandra. Dad found her cane among a cluster of rhododendrons. The swans sailed placidly in the distance, near a small island in the lake where a willow tree grew among wild yellow irises.

It was still light when the divers tumbled over the sides of their boats into the water and disappeared.

It was dark when the next-door neighbor took me home.

It was noon the next day when the police said Alexandra was not in the lake and not in the park. She had been abducted.

It was September when one of the neighbors whispered that perhaps Mom and Dad had done something to Alexandra. Mom had been at the hairdresser and Dad had been in a meeting all that day, and eighteen people said so. But the whispers spread. My friends' didn't come to the house any longer. October seeped into November, and on a cold windy day, my mother fell apart. She came to my school and took me out of class, crying and incoherent. I returned to school later in the week, but no one came near me. Girls who had been my friends kept a careful distance, and when I passed them, they whispered audibly, and sometimes one or another would stifle laughter. The neighbors watched us, but no one came to see us. We had graduated from being victims to being untouchable.

What is the name of this terrible, lonely place?

One year, two years, three years. My father calls the police every Monday morning and every Thursday afternoon. Our swan is gone.

Tell me the name of this terrible place. It must be worse than Forever.

"I hate your neighbors," Tasha says. "I'd like to kill your rotten neighbors. You should move away."

"We can't," I say helplessly. "Don't you see? Alexandra might come home and we'd be gone."

Tasha crawls up on the lawn swing with me and hugs me hard. "Do you think she still might come home?" she asks.

"I thought she had," I say.

On Thursday of that week, while Mom and Ben are reading on the deck, someone rings the front doorbell. I open the door to find a short woman wearing heavy makeup, with stiff hair the same color as Ben's plastic duck.

"Who are you?" she demands. "Are you one of the Deacons?"

A bearded man stands at the bottom of the steps, slightly to one side, and he holds a camera behind him, as if he's ashamed of what he wants to do. I've seen cameras like that before.

I've seen this cartoon of a woman before, too. I close the door in her face.

"We're going to talk about Alexandra again," she shouts through the door. "Doesn't your mother have something she'd like to say to us? We can help, you know. Maybe your sister will see our program and call you to let you know she's all right. Isn't that what you want? Don't you care about Alexandra anymore?"

I rush to the phone, try to dial my dad's work number, but I make a mistake and have to dial again. The doorbell rings persistently, madly, as if something has gone wrong with it and it can't stop. Morgan circles the room, protesting hoarsely.

Dad's assistant says he's in a meeting. "Tell him to come home right now!" I cry. "Tell him it's an emergency!"

The doorbell rings again and again. Now the woman shouts, "Don't you want to tell your side of it? I'm willing to listen, you know. Nora Deacon, are you there? Nora, aren't you interested in getting your daughter back? Nora? Nora?"

Mom comes in, holding Ben. Her eyes glitter with purpose.

I grab her arm to stop her from opening the door. "Don't," I say. "Don't let them scare Ben. Take him upstairs and shut the bedroom door. I've called Dad, and now I'm going to call Gran."

"I know you're in there!" the lunatic on the porch yells.

"Mom, take Ben upstairs!" I say. "You don't want them to see him, to put him on TV."

Ben is crying now. Mom takes him away quickly, shielding his head with one hand, as if someone was trying to strike him. Morgan leaps at me, certain that I'll catch him. I do.

Alexandra follows me anxiously, wringing her hands. "What is this place?" she begs. "I don't know this place." I use the kitchen phone to call Gran and then I go upstairs to Alexandra's room and lie on her bed with my face in her pillow. Downstairs, the racket goes on and on.

I hear my parents' air conditioner start up, and then their TV. Mom is playing Ben's *Teletubbies* tape for him.

Morgan kneads Alexandra's quilt, but he isn't purring. Someone is banging on the glass patio door downstairs under my room, and shouting.

I can't stand any more. How can things like this happen? What did we ever do to bring this down on us?

I use the hall phone to call Father Carrington. He answers the phone himself. I guess the God business isn't very brisk today.

"Where is God?" I shout. "You tell me where He is *right now*!"

There's a pause. Then he says, "Turn around and look, Skylar. He's there. Are you home? What's happened? Who's there with you?"

"Not God," I say.

"Your mother and Ben? Tell your mother I'll be there as soon as I can."

"Dad and Gran are coming," I say. "That's enough. There's no room for anybody else."

"Skylar," he says. "Don't go into Alexandra's room. Promise me."

But Alexandra is beckoning me from her doorway. "Hurry," she says.

I hang up.

The phone rings immediately, but I go into my sister's room and close the door behind me.

chapter
ELEVEN

From Alexandra's window, I watch the horror show. Gran arrives first, stopping her car in the street because the driveway is blocked by the TV station's van. The yellow-haired troll charges my grandmother's car. Gran doesn't get out. The man with the camera hovers, first in front of the car and then behind the troll, as if he's afraid of Gran. He should be. The phone in the hall rings, and I answer, sure it will be Gran, calling from her cell phone.

"Is everybody all right?" Gran shouts over the background noise. The troll is screeching unintelligibly now. She and my grandmother have always hated each other. "I've called the police," Gran tells me. "They're coming."

I hang up and run back to the window. The troll and her companion have moved back into our yard again. Gran waits in her car. I wait, too, kneeling on Alexandra's window seat. I'm both angry and terrified, wanting to run away, if only there were a place where I'd be safe.

Two police cars arrive swiftly, silently. Troll scuttles out of our yard, with the cameraman behind her, heading toward their van. Two officers get out and talk to them. One leans against the van, a big hand resting on his hip. The other walks out to Gran's car and she rolls down her window.

"Let's not look anymore," Alexandra says. "The troll woman is from the Poison Glen."

I remember Gran's story about the Poison Glen filled with dead and dying trees, where all dark things come from. The creatures of the Poison Glen call to us, to lure us, and if we go, we can never escape.

Alexandra and I pull her old toy chest out from the back of her closet, and we play dolls, sitting on the carpet where the magic colors fall. No darkness, no wicked voices, can come through the window where the suncatcher hangs.

"You be Betsy's mother and I'll be Julie's mother," Alexandra says. "We'll have a picnic here under the trees, and then we'll feed the swans."

I see the swans floating in the distance, placid and stately, watching their own reflections in the calm lake.

"Oh, my darling girl," Gran says. She kneels beside me and gathers me into her arms. I see Father Carrington over her shoulder. He is wearing his black clothes, but he has tears in his eyes.

Now I have pills to take, and so does Mom, but they are different. Our family doctor gave me white ones, and Mom's are green.

Dad canceled our cable service, so we don't have live TV anymore.

We watch comedy videos sometimes, and Gran keeps Ben provided with children's cartoons and nature films. The rest of the time, Gran plays classical music on the stereo.

I stay home from school for a few days. This is necessary because I begin crying without warning. I don't seem to have any control over it, and that scares Ben. In my best moments, I'm socially unacceptable, somewhat like my mother.

Gran is staying with us now, sleeping in the bedroom that might be Ben's someday. Ben is ecstatic and trails around after her all day. She has managed to housebreak him, too, and now he uses the bathroom most of the time, although he has also flushed two washcloths and Morgan's collar. Morgan didn't like it anyway.

My mother stays in bed.

The girls from school call, but I don't talk much except to Tasha. "I'm in the Poison Glen," I told her the first time. "I'll call you if I ever get out." I was crying again, so I suppose she knew I was crazier than ever.

She didn't wait for me though. Every day after school she calls, to tell me about class and what D.J.'s sister paints on his neck—butterflies and lizards and Cleopatra's eyes. I want to go back to class! I want to be a part of real life, not this dark half life on the edge of everything. But I can't stop crying.

As I slowly get hold of myself, Gran takes care of everything. She has even cleared out Alexandra's room. The closet is empty and the bed is stripped. Even the suncatcher is gone, and the books are packed in boxes.

The night before I go back to school, I look for Alexandra's journal and find it at the bottom of one of the boxes. I sit down on the bare mattress and press the journal against my chest. What will I find? What did she write? Will I learn what happened to her that day?

It's blank.

I turn every page, looking for something, even a single word, a message, a hint that she is still here. Or was here. Or would have been here if she could.

A sign.

"You can have my journal," Alexandra says. She is sitting on the window seat, dangling her legs. I see the long angry scar on the front of her ankle.

"Does it still hurt?" I ask.

She shakes her head and her silky hair swings forward, then swings back again to reveal her fifteen-year-old face.

"Where did you go that day?" I ask. She knows what day I mean.

"You don't want me to answer that," she says.

She's right. I don't want to know. But yet I *must* know. She went to feed the swans, and—and then? *And then?*

"Can you ever come back?" I ask.

But she's gone again. I wanted an answer to my question, but I know with a sudden terrible pain that I will never get it. I put the journal back in the box and leave my sister's room.

This is August eighteenth, the anniversary, exactly three years from the day she went to feed the swans. Gran is playing a comedy video in the living room, rocking drowsy Ben in her lap. "I think we'll have spaghetti tonight," she tells me when I walk through on my way to the den.

"Good," I say. I turn on the computer and play Solitaire until dinnertime. Once I hear my mother say, "I can't bear not knowing," but

I turn on the small stereo in the den to drown out her suffering. I can't bear not knowing either.

The next morning on the way to the bus stop I see the crows playing over my head, tumbling in the wind. They have invented some sort of game. I stop to watch for a moment, but they pay no attention to me.

At school I find my friends sitting on the steps. I missed five classes, but it seems as if I had been here yesterday. Margaret's hair is curlier, Naomi has a bad sunburn, Tasha is wearing gorgeous silver earrings, D.J. is adorned with a ring of small goldfish swimming around his tanned neck, and Shawn has bandages on both knees.

"What happened to you?" I ask him.

"Flipped off my skateboard," he says. "How are *you*?"

"I had food poisoning," I tell him. "But I'm fine now." I had eaten a meal in the Poison Glen, I think.

Tasha links her arm with mine. "You're looking good," she says. "Are we doing something after class?"

"Hamburgers?" I ask.

Everybody yells, "Yes!" They're too glad to see me and I cringe inside. Do they pity me? Will I become too much of a burden, me with my broken heart?

On the way upstairs to class, Tasha whispers, "Margaret saw it on TV and told the others. They were really sorry for your family."

I keep climbing, climbing. I can do this. I'm strong, like Gran.

When I walk into class, Mrs. Vargas stops me. "I've got a stack of work for you," she says. "If you complete it all by the end of the course, you'll still get a decent grade." She doesn't mention that Gran called her and explained, if it's possible to explain.

I take the folder and loose papers she hands me. "I'll finish it," I promise. I will, too. I haven't come this far to fail.

She touches my arm, then squeezes it gently. "You write beautiful papers," she says. "But you've heard that before."

I nod and take my seat. Jenny smiles carefully and says, "I hope you're better."

"I'm fine," I say heartily.

Mrs. Vargas has closed the door, and I look up at the grimy window, expecting to see Alexandra watching. No one is there. I settle down in my seat, anticipating what Mrs. Vargas will read today. I'll focus on that and let everything else wait for another time. Or maybe I'll never deal with those other things.

After class, I call Gran and tell her that I'm having lunch with my friends. "How is Mom?" I ask, expecting to hear her say, "Just the same."

There's a moment of silence, passing so quickly that I almost don't catch it. "She's resting upstairs," Gran says. "Have a good time." She hangs up on me.

"Done?" Tasha asks when I tuck my cell phone back in my pocket. "I should be so lucky that any phone conversation with my family would end that fast. My mother never misses a chance to remind me about my 'shortcomings.'"

Margaret giggles and nods. Naomi rolls her eyes in sympathy.

"Are we going, or are we standing here for the rest of our lives comparing families?" D.J. demands.

"Let's go," I say, and we start up the block toward the place that makes good hamburgers. D.J. walks next to me, and I see that his sister painted a small goldfish on the back of his left hand, too.

"What does your sister want to do when she finishes with art school?" I ask.

"She wants to draw cartoons," he says.

"And what about you?" I ask. I catch myself actually being interested, and not just asking questions so that I don't have to talk.

He shrugs. "That's a million years away."

"Do you draw pictures on your sister's neck and hands?" I ask.

He laughs, looks down at me, and looks away again. "Yeah, sure. Not if I want to stay alive . . ." He stops talking. "I'm sorry," he says. "God, I hate myself."

"It's okay," I say, doing my best to sound supportive. I'm sorry for him. What are you supposed to say to someone like me? For the first time I understand how hard it is to have a friend whose family has lost someone the way we lost Alexandra. Everybody knows someone who has lost a family member to death, and we see them grieve and stumble on. But my family lost someone to emptiness, not death. We had no ceremony, no grave, no headstone. We had the squawkings and clackings of the TV trolls. "Tell us." "Did she." "Was she." "Won't she."

"Do you miss your sister?" That's what the yellow troll asked me once. She plunged at me from behind the neighbor's hedge, holding out her evil wand, and someone swung a video camera toward me. I ran, but she scuttled behind me. Gran opened the front door and snatched me inside. "If you come back, I'll shoot you like a mad dog," Gran shouted at the yellow troll.

We order hamburgers again. D.J. hangs his left arm over the back of the booth so that it's almost around me. "Take some of my fries," he says. "You need to eat more."

"I eat enough," I say, but I take several of his fries anyway. I'd like to lean against him, but I won't. Across the booth, Tasha grins at me. She read my mind, the way good friends do.

Afterward, everyone waits at the bus stop with Naomi and me, and when the bus finally comes, it interrupts Shawn in the middle of a story about his four dogs. Tasha says, "Tomorrow, Skylar."

"I'll see you guys tomorrow," I say.

When I get home, I find Dad leading Mom out to the car. She pays no attention to me, but instead watches her feet as she walks. Her hair isn't combed. She holds her blue cardigan closed with a shaking hand.

"What's going on?" I ask.

Gran, holding silent, staring Ben, says, "Your mom's going to the hospital for a little checkup."

I blink. "Mom?"

She doesn't answer me. Dad turns and says, "Mind your grandmother, kids," and helps Mom into the passenger seat of his car. She covers her eyes with one hand while he fastens her seat belt. Then he puts the suitcase I hadn't seen before into the trunk and slams it shut.

"She's staying at the hospital?" I ask Gran incredulously.

Gran bustles me inside and closes the door. "For a little while. A few days, maybe. We'll see how it goes."

"But why?" I ask as I put my papers and folder on the hall table.

Gran stops and looks at the closed door for a moment. Ben rests his head against her shoulder. "Your mother needs more help than we can give her here. Ted took her to the doctor this morning, and it was decided—*they* decided—that this is the best thing to do now."

"But what's *wrong* with her?" I cry. Ben flinches and hides his face from me against her sweatshirt.

"Your mother is having a nervous breakdown," Gran says simply. Ben clutches her around the neck, but I know he doesn't understand what she said. I don't understand, either.

"Is she going to be all right?" I ask. What am I supposed to do without my mother? I don't have a sister. Where is the end of it? How many people will I lose before this is over?

"Give Ben to me," I say, and I hold out my arms. Gran gives him to me and I cuddle him close. "I love you, Ben," I whisper against his sweet neck.

"I love you, Ben," Alexandra says, weeping in the doorway between the living room and the family room. She's fading now. Only her eyes are still bright. "I love you, Skylar," she says.

"Other one sis," Ben murmurs, pointing at her.

Gran turns to look where he is pointing and asks, "What did he say? I didn't hear him."

"He wants a nap in the family room," I say, and I carry him through the doorway, but our sister is gone again. I sit on the couch with Ben's head in my lap and pull the woolly afghan over him.

"Sing," he demands.

I sing the purple dinosaur song, and Ben closes his eyes. Morgan jumps up and curls himself into a ball against Ben's chest. Ben idly tugs on the cat's whiskers, and Morgan purrs idiotically.

Outside the window, the beech tree stirs in the warm August

wind. Summer school will be over soon. The birds will fly south. Autumn will blow across us and winter will punish us. I know the name of this place. I always knew. The name of this terrible place is Skylar's Life.

I smooth Ben's silky hair and whisper, "Little brother."

Father Carrington comes later in the afternoon, wearing his clerical clothes again. Ben is up from his nap, playing weird music on his xylophone. He smiles at the priest, digs through the toys piled around him, and extracts part of a graham cracker, which he offers. Father Carrington declines politely, so Ben pounds the cracker into crumbs with his plastic hammers and goes back to composing his opus.

Father Carrington sits down opposite me, hunching himself into as small a space as possible. "I saw your mother briefly," he says.

"How is she?" I ask. My mouth is dry.

"She'd been given something to help her sleep," he said. "She didn't say much. She worries about Ben and you."

"When is Dad coming home?" I ask. I wonder if he's going to stay at the hospital with Mom, leaving Ben and me with Gran. What kind of family is this?

"He said he'd be home for dinner." The priest spreads his hands out over his knees and studies them with interest. Then he looks up at me and says, "It's time for you to talk to someone else. I'm not the best help for you at a time like this."

"I won't talk to anyone else, so forget it," I say flatly. "Dr. Johnson said I can talk to you instead of a psychiatrist. I don't even need the pills anymore."

"But you *don't* talk to me," he says. "We only go in circles. You need somebody better."

"I won't talk to someone who doesn't believe in God."

He sighs. "You can ask a psychiatrist or psychologist if he does. I'm sure your father doesn't want you to see someone you don't like."

"Did Dad say I have to see someone else?" I ask suspiciously. I don't like the idea that they've been talking about me behind my back.

"No. But I think it would be best. I'm not helping you. Perhaps a woman would be better for you."

I snicker without meaning to. "Just in case God really is a woman after all?" I ask.

"You can be so exasperating."

"So you're firing me," I say. I'm beginning to panic now, but I can't let him know. I don't want him to know that I need him—and might even need God.

"No, no, no. I'm trying to do what's best for you," he says.

"I'll see you next Wednesday at the same time," I say. "Unless I decide to go somewhere with my friends after class." I can't resist making sure he understands that he isn't my first priority, that I have options, other places to go, other places I just might *want* to go.

Gran brings him a cup of coffee, but he asks if he can drink it in the kitchen with her and follows her out of the room. I grin to myself and smooth Ben's hair. He's snoring faintly and I love the sound.

Through the window, I see Alexandra walking under the beech tree and away from us.

❧

On Saturday, Dad takes me to the hospital to see Mom. She sits in a chair looking out a window at an ugly tree with purple leaves. Her hair has been brushed straight back, and I find it hard to recognize her.

I kneel beside the chair. "How are you, Mom?" I ask.

She turns her face and smiles a little at me, but she's only being polite. I'm afraid that she doesn't know who I am.

I tell her about Ben, but she's looking at the purple tree again. I understand how consoling a tree can be, but I wish hers were prettier. After a while I give up and go out to the hall to wait for Dad. I can't dwell on the situation because I can't imagine how it can end—or even if it will end.

Father Carrington shuffles along the hall, carrying his prayer book. He blinks with surprise when he sees me.

"Are you going to see Mom?" I ask.

"Yes, your mother and someone else, too," he says.

"Big business for the loony bin this week," I say. I can't help being angry. "But it's not so big for God, I guess."

He looks up with that "Give me a break" look. "God's always available," he says. "Even for an argument. Did you visit with your mother?"

"She didn't say anything," I say, suddenly blinking away tears. "I don't know if she recognizes me."

"She's waiting for Alexandra," he says, and he shuffles away sadly.

"I'm not!" I say to his back. "Not anymore. God didn't keep His part of the bargain."

Father Carrington comes back, like an interested vulture. "You never asked Him what His part of the bargain was."

"I didn't care," I say. "I only wanted to keep my sister."

"She was never yours." He shuffles away again, and this time I don't call him back.

I stare dry-eyed at a print on the wall. It's hanging crooked. Life, I think, and I'm afraid that I'm going to laugh insanely and end up in the empty bed across the hall from Mom. By the time I have control of myself, Dad comes out and says it's time to leave.

"Why don't we pick up pizza for dinner?" Dad says as if everything is all right, as if we're on our way home from a shopping trip and too tired to fix dinner.

"Let's get soft ice cream, too," I say.

On the way home, I see a pretty girl in a long pink dress, walking with a boy. She smiles when she sees me looking at her and I smile back, and then I bite my lip. I know now I won't see Alexandra again, and I'll never learn any more about her, either. She is a lost book, a letter written but never delivered, a half-told story and the story-teller has died.

chapter
TWELVE

On the day before summer school ends, Margaret gives a party at her house after class. The five of us walk home with her and find that her mother has set up a picnic for us on the patio under a large maple tree.

"Your yard is beautiful!" I tell Mrs. Green, and I mean it. The place looks like the photos I see in Mom's gardening magazines. It invites me to take a walk and investigate this small grove of trees, that rock garden, and then the lily pond with a fountain and goldfish.

Mrs. Green gently taps the stone face of an ornament hanging on the house. "He's called the Green Man," she says. "I gave my garden to him the day we moved into the house, and he keeps it growing for us." The stone face, wreathed with leaves, smiles upon the garden and my friends.

Mrs. Green and her Green Man. Mom will love this. I'll tell her the next time I visit her. Maybe I'll even get her a Green Man of her own.

"I'm Irish," she says, but I had already guessed that from her accent. "We believe that living things can use a bit of help from here and there."

"My grandmother's mother was from County Kerry," I tell her.

Her smile widens. "I was born in Kerry," she says. "I'd like to meet your grandmother." She slips her hand under my chin and lifts it. "Just look at those eyes," she says. "My dad would have said that God put them in with a sooty finger."

D.J., watching, says, "What does that mean?" He sounds faintly indignant, as if Mrs. Green insulted me.

"It means she's got black eyelashes," Mrs. Green says. "It's unusual for a blond, but I'm sure you've thought that yourself."

"Who, me?" D.J. asks. He ducks his head and walks away, heading toward the table of food.

"Not so young, but not old enough yet," Mrs. Green says softly, laughing. I laugh, too, embarrassed for him.

When the phone in the house rings, Mrs. Green goes inside and I hear her talking to someone. I wonder about her son, the one who died from leukemia. The Green Man smiles at the world in spite of it. Gardens grow anyway. My friends are laughing about something, and Tasha calls out, "Hey, Skylar, are you going to eat or are you just going to watch?"

I join them and fill my plate as high as Shawn's. We sit at another table, a long wooden one under a grape arbor, and a squirrel watches us intently from the edge of a birdbath.

"Don't feed him," Margaret warns us. "He's getting too bold." The squirrel shakes his tail angrily, as if he understood.

We've just finished eating when the first rain spatters us, and before we've gathered up the last of the food and taken it inside, a storm roars down, hurling sheets of water and thunder. D.J. and Shawn bring in the remaining bowls, and we watch the rain while we snack on the last of the sandwiches.

"You can't leave food on the plates," Mrs. Green tells us. "It's bad luck."

"I thought we were always supposed to leave a bite on each plate for the fairies," Margaret protests.

"That's my *other* story," Mrs. Green says placidly.

I watch the rain and the yard, and I wonder if Margaret's brother ever walks there. Does he watch the house from the arbor? Does he play with the spoiled squirrel?

No. He's not caught here the way I caught Alexandra. And I would still pull her back if I could.

Mrs. Green takes all of us home in the storm, and D.J., seeing my house, says, "You've got an easy address to remember."

"I guess you'll have to prove that," I say, surprising myself. "I guess you'll have to come and see me sometime."

"We'll all come," Naomi says, and everyone agrees.

The last day in class is both happy and sad. Mrs. Vargas tells us that everybody passed, but she won't say more than that. I let out the breath I was holding, and next to me, Jenny slides down in her seat and whispers, "Yes!"

"If you learned anything here," Mrs. Vargas says, "I hope it was respect for short stories and poetry, and especially for your own opinions."

Most of the kids nod.

"Read," she says. "Read as if your lives depend on it, because they do. Read to learn and to have fun, but most of all, read for selfish reasons." She smiles and shakes her head. "Oh, if I could only convince you to read for selfish reasons."

We're dismissed, and most of us hang around until she tell us that she has to lock the room. My friends and I linger outside under the trees, reluctant to say good-bye. I'm not the only one who is afraid to let go.

"Let's promise not to lose track of each other," Tasha says. "We could get together on a Saturday sometimes and do something fun."

"With all the trouble I'm still having with my transcripts, I'll be back here next summer, taking something else," Shawn says. "Gotta go, people. Give me a call, D.J." He lopes away and doesn't look back.

"I've got an appointment for a physical—I'm turning out for the swim team," D.J. says. He stalls around, first watching his feet and then the sky. Finally he holds out his notebook. "Here, write down your phone numbers. I'll call all of you. And you can call me. We'll get together, and old Shawn will show up, too."

We write our names and numbers in his notebook and he writes his in ours. Finally we can't put it off any longer. Two buses have gone by and Naomi is complaining that we'll have to stand up all the way downtown again.

She and I watch the others leave and then run for the bus. "This has been so much fun," she tells me. She looks as if she's ready to cry. "I'll miss seeing everybody every day. I'll even miss Mrs. Vargas. Can you believe that?"

"It was the best English class I ever had," I say.

I'm reading to Ben in the backyard, late in the afternoon, when Gran comes out and tells me I have guests. I turn the slave driver over to her and run inside. I half expect to see Tasha, even though she didn't call.

Tasha, Margaret, and Naomi are waiting in the living room. When I come in, they mumble hello, then look around the room uncomfortably.

"Hey," I say. "What's going on?"

Tasha wears a guilty expression and looks at everyone but at me. Naomi is holding something behind her back and she seems fascinated with the cover of a book on the coffee table. Margaret smiles, clearly embarrassed.

"I told them about the swans," Tasha says finally. "I hope you aren't mad."

"It's such a beautiful story," Margaret says. "The swans and . . . and . . ."

Naomi holds out a plastic sack. "Bread," she says. "We thought we'd go to the lake and feed the swans with you."

I'm so astonished that I can't speak. What possessed them to do something like this?

"I don't know if they're still there," I say finally. I'm not certain that I want to find out, either.

"They're there," Tasha says. "We went to the lake first, and there are four swans by the island. We saw them."

"We thought we'd take you there, and you could call them . . ." Naomi holds the sack behind her back again. I can see that she's expecting the worst.

"Come with us," Tasha says. "Come with us, Skylar. We'll feed the swans, and everything will be all right."

I blink away tears. "I'll tell Gran that I'll be gone for a while."

"We'll wait outside for you," Margaret says, and she escapes out the door first, with Naomi close behind. Tasha smiles, to encourage me.

Gran, busy with Ben, barely looks up when I tell her I'm going out for a walk with my friends. When I join the others on the sidewalk, the curtains on the neighbor's window stir. Tasha sees and makes a face.

"I really do hate your neighbors," Tasha says loudly, defiantly. She's outrageous, and I can't remember when I've liked anyone more. "Somebody's been watching us ever since we came out here," she complains in her big voice. "We thought about mooning her, but we didn't want to upset your grandmother."

Margaret and Naomi laugh, and Tasha says, "Hey, I'm only expressing my opinion, okay? I got a B in English so I must be doing something right. Let's go."

We head toward the lake, two by two on the sidewalk. Naomi swings the sack of bread. I don't see my crows anywhere, but we pass a birch tree filled with starlings imitating sparrows while they trade branches.

"You know what four swans remind me of?" Margaret asks. "The Children of Lir."

"I know that story," Naomi says eagerly. "I used to have a picture book about them."

Tasha and I don't know the story, and Margaret volunteers to tell it.

"It's about a king's beautiful children who were turned into swans by their evil stepmother," she says. "They stayed swans for nine hundred years before someone broke the spell, but then they weren't children anymore. They were old instead."

"Well, that's a horrible story!" Tasha complains.

"Oh, Irish stories are always horrible," Margaret says, laughing now. "Half the time my mother's stories scared me to death and the rest of the time I thought they were wonderful. I'll tell you what— the Children of Lir should have stayed swans forever. They wanted the spell to be broken and they sang about it wherever they went, so somebody finally turned them back into people again. But they were better off swimming or flying."

"Alexandra said that swans spend most of their lives on water or in the air, because they're so clumsy on land," I say. "They don't like being earthbound." My sister had been earthbound because of her ankle. And then because of me.

Now I see a crow sitting on a street sign. "Graawk," he says. It seems to be a passing remark, the bird equivalent of Ben's "Hey!"

"I'm crazy about crows," Naomi says as she stops to admire him. "One stole my uncle's latte once. He bought a cup in one of the mall coffee shops and took it outside to the parking lot and put it down on the hood of his car while he unlocked the door. A crow came down and picked it up by the rim and flew away with it. Honestly! I know it's true because he was so mad that he stopped by our house to tell us about it. I can't stand him, so I had to run to my bedroom to laugh."

She throws a piece of bread to the crow and he drops down, grabs it, and flies away.

"I hope that was the same crow," she says seriously.

"No, I think that's one of mine," I say. "They follow me to the bus stop in the morning. Sometimes they're scary."

"They won't be following you anymore," Margaret says. "School's out, remember?"

"Oh, I wish it wasn't over yet!" I exclaim. "This really was the best time I ever had."

"Haven't you ever been to Disneyland?" Naomi says. "Trust me, it's more fun than summer school."

But Tasha smiles at me in a way that lets me know she understands exactly what I mean. We cross the last street before the park, hurrying a little now. We still have a long way to go to the place where the swans live. A line of joggers takes up the path, so we walk on the sunburned grass, past the children's playground, past the swimming beach, and past the grove of ancient madronas, until we see the island with its nodding willow tree. We walk out to the point.

I don't see the swans. A dozen mallard ducks waddle toward us, quacking instructions about the bread they suspect we have in the sack.

"Don't give them any bread," Tasha says. "Look how fat they are! If they had to fly, I don't think they could do it."

143

"Where did you see the swans?" I say.

"They were between us and the island before," Margaret says. "Right there." She points at the choppy gray water.

"Whistle like Alexandra did," Tasha says.

I'm not sure I can do it. My lips feel stiff. Even if I can whistle, the swans wouldn't remember after all this time. Perhaps they aren't even the same swans. If I call them and they don't come, then I'll feel worse than I already do. I shouldn't be here. I should thank my friends and tell them I just can't go on with this. I understand what they're trying to do, but the ceremony can only work if the swans come. If they remember my sister.

"Let's move back so she can be here alone," Tasha tells the others. "Let her have the sack. Maybe if we're not standing right here watching, they'll come."

They move away to the other side of the jogging path. The ducks follow them, filled with noisy hope. I wait, and after a while I see one swan sailing out from behind the island.

Alexandra, help me, I think. But she's not here.

I whistle once, and then I start crying. Is there ever going to be an end to tears? It takes a while for me to calm myself, and then I try again.

The swan seems to hesitate. Three others join it. They watch me, but they don't come nearer.

I step forward, close to the water's edge, and whistle again.

Now they come. Now they sail toward me, their white wings held out from their sides, stiffly curved. I don't care about my sneakers, so I step out into the water and wait for them.

They swim straight to me, and I take two steps back to shore. They struggle to the grass, clumsy now. I scatter some of the bread in front of them and I can't stop smiling. They remember my sister.

I hold out more bread to them and they take it from me, pinching my fingers sometimes. I hear the ducks coming complaining angrily about favoritism and the three tricksters who led them astray. I toss bread to them to keep them away from the swans, who still feed from my free hand.

When the meal is nearly over, three of the swans go back to the water, but one stays near me, and when the ducks get too close, the swan opens her beak and raises her wings threateningly. I whistle the three notes again, and she studies me closely.

I have one bit of bread left, and I hold it out to her. She takes it daintily, and then, with one last look at my face, she returns to the water. She floats a few feet away, still watching me. Then suddenly the other three swans take flight. I look up. Oh, they are beautiful, white against the pearl gray sky.

The last swan lifts up from the water and joins them. Alexandra told me once that they spend their nights on Puget Sound, where they're safe from predators. I watch until I can't see them any longer, and then I turn and climb the gentle slope to my friends who waited so patiently. I drop the plastic bag in a trash can as I pass.

"They remembered," Margaret says. Her voice breaks.

"Come on, we'll walk you home," Tasha tells me, and we start back the way we came. Wind ruffles the lake and the trees around it. The reeds flutter and hiss. I can smell the sharp scent of the wild peppermint that grows near the water.

At the playground, the swings are deserted, and they, too, blow in the wind restlessly. There are four new blue plastic seats, flanked by two yellow ones, and they sit over a large bed of scuffed sand.

"Let's swing!" Margaret says. "I haven't done it for years and years." Before I can protest, she runs across the sand and sits on one of the blue seats. "Come on, everybody." Reluctantly, I follow her.

The swings are low for us, especially Tasha. She laughs while she folds herself up to fit, with her knees practically under her chin. Margaret and Naomi push off, bending forward and then leaning back, climbing higher.

Is the wind pushing me or holding me back? I don't know and it doesn't matter, because I'm ready for it. Suddenly I'm enthusiastic, glad to be here, and I lean back as far as I can and stretch out my legs. The ropes sting my hands and I dare to loosen my grip a little. These swings aren't as tall as the ones I played on when I was a child, or perhaps they only seem smaller because I've grown up. I never went this high, though. I've never soared like this because I never had the courage. Now I see the joggers on the path and the ducks nibbling along the shore. Now I see everything.

I don't realize how high I've gone until I hear Tasha say, "You cheat, Skylar. You do this all the time."

"Honestly, I don't," I say. I let myself slow down gradually, and when I get off the swing I rub my burning hands on my jeans.

"How about getting together again?" Naomi says. "Once a month on a Saturday? And in between, we can talk on the phone."

"I like that idea," Margaret says. "Maybe we can have a sleepover at my place before fall semester starts."

"We can go to movies," Tasha says.

"If we ever have real boyfriends, we could all go out together on a quadruple date," Naomi says.

The rest of us laugh at this fanciful idea. "Sure we will," Tasha scoffs. "When pigs fly."

"Oinker Airline Flight Two-ten, loading at the gate," I say. "Anything is possible."

We stop walking to laugh, bent over, helpless. We're offending the serious joggers and the power walkers, but we don't care.

I can be brave, because the swans are floating safe on the Sound. I don't need to see them to know that this is true.

Jean Thesman has written several award-winning novels for young adults. She is a member of both the Authors Guild and the Society for Children's Book Writers and Illustrators (SCBWI).

She lives in Washington State, the setting for most of her books.